FOX RIVER VALLEY PLD

3 1783 00494 0940

 W9-AUA-245

Fox River Valley PLD
555 Barrington Ave., Dundee, IL 60118
www.frvpld.info
Renew online or call 847-590-8706

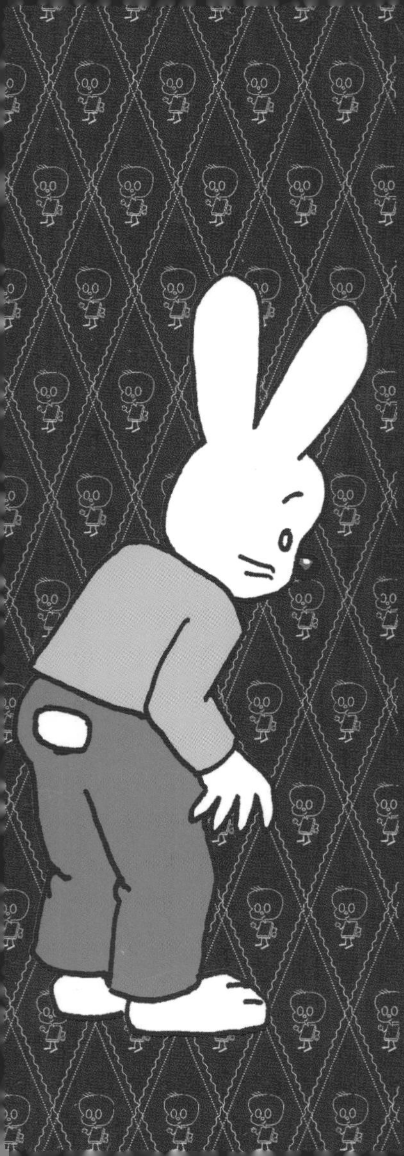

JACK AND THE BOX

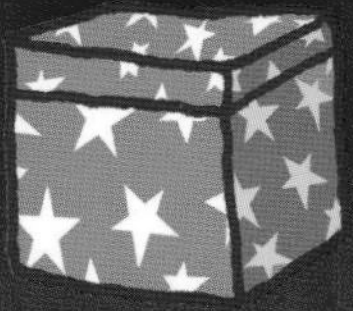

art spiegelman

JACK AND THE BOX

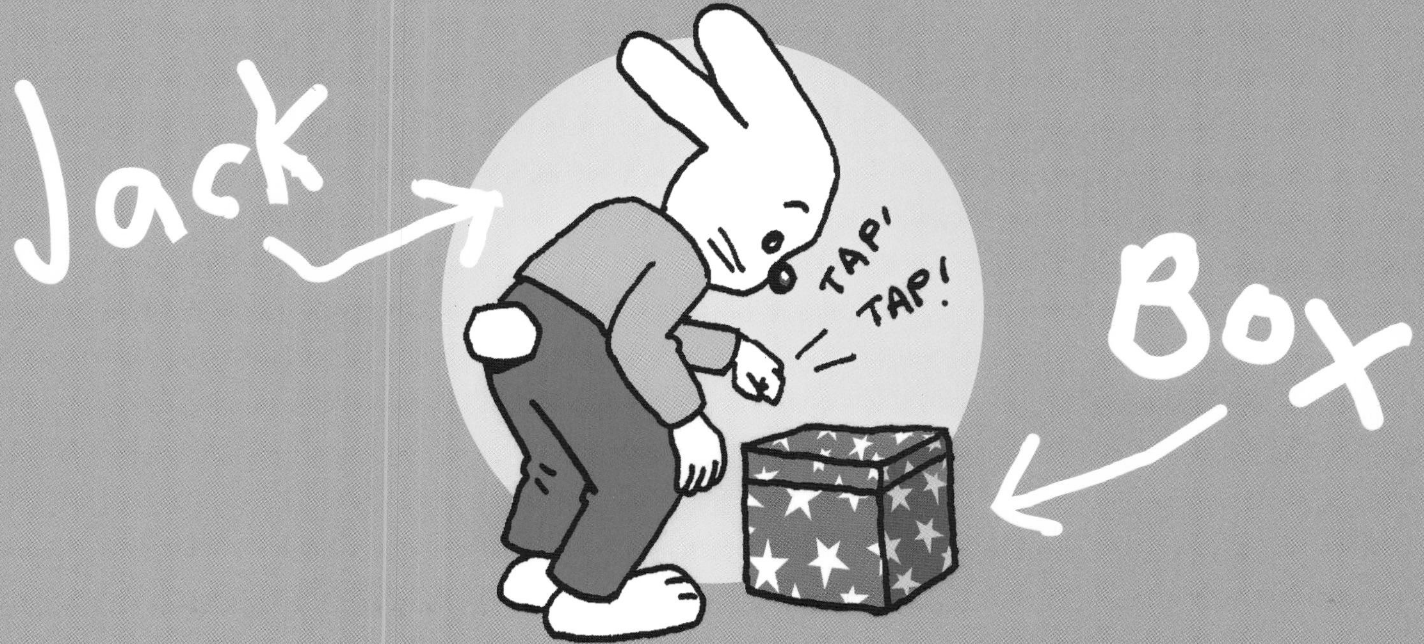
Jack
TAP!
TAP!
Box

A TOON BOOK BY

art spiegelman

TOON BOOKS IS AN IMPRINT OF CANDLEWICK PRESS

Visit us at www.abdopublishing.com

Reinforced library bound editions published in 2014 by Spotlight, a division of the ABDO Group, PO Box 398166, Minneapolis, MN 55439. Spotlight produces high-quality reinforced library bound editions for schools and libraries.
Reprinted by agreement with Raw Junior, LLC. All rights reserved.

Printed in the United States of America, North Mankato, Minnesota.
042013
092013
♻ This book contains at least 10% recycled material.

Editorial Director: Françoise Mouly. Advisor: Art Spiegelman.
Book Design: Françoise Mouly, Jonathan Bennett & Art Spiegelman.

Library of Congress Cataloging-in-Publication Data
This book was previously cataloged with the following information:

Spiegelman, Art.
Jack and the box : a toon book / by Art Spiegelman.
  p. cm. -- (TOON Books)
Summary: A rabbit named Jack receives a jack-in-the-box as a present from his parents, but this spring-loaded device is a mere silly toy.
[1. Rabbits --Fiction. 2. Jack-in-the-box --Fiction. 3. Toys --Fiction. 4. Comic books, strips, etc., 5. Graphic novels.]

2007910340

ISBN 978-1-61479-151-5 (reinforced library bound edition)

All Spotlight books are reinforced library bindings
and manufactured in the United States of America.

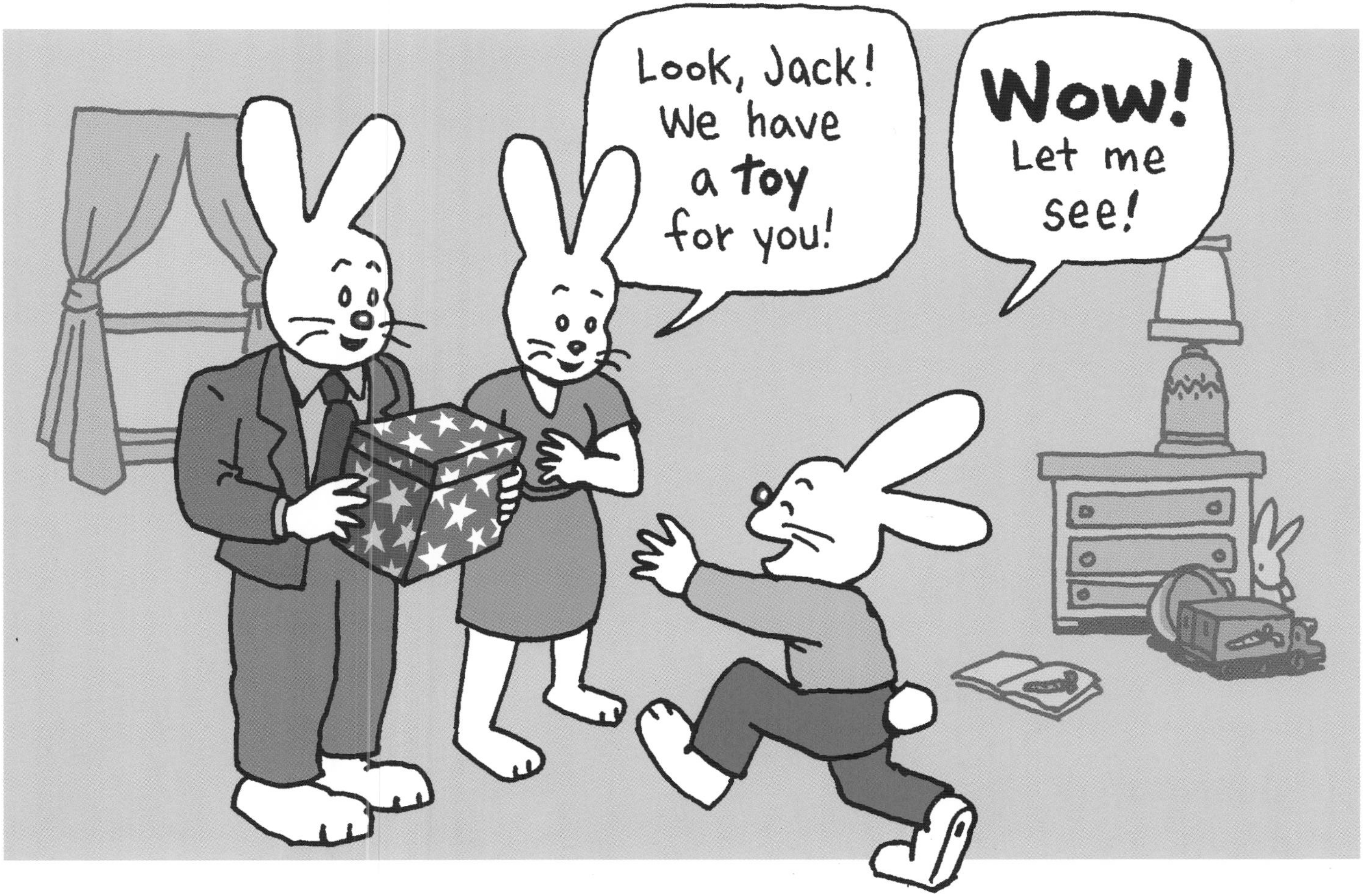
Look, Jack! We have a **toy** for you!
Wow! Let me see!

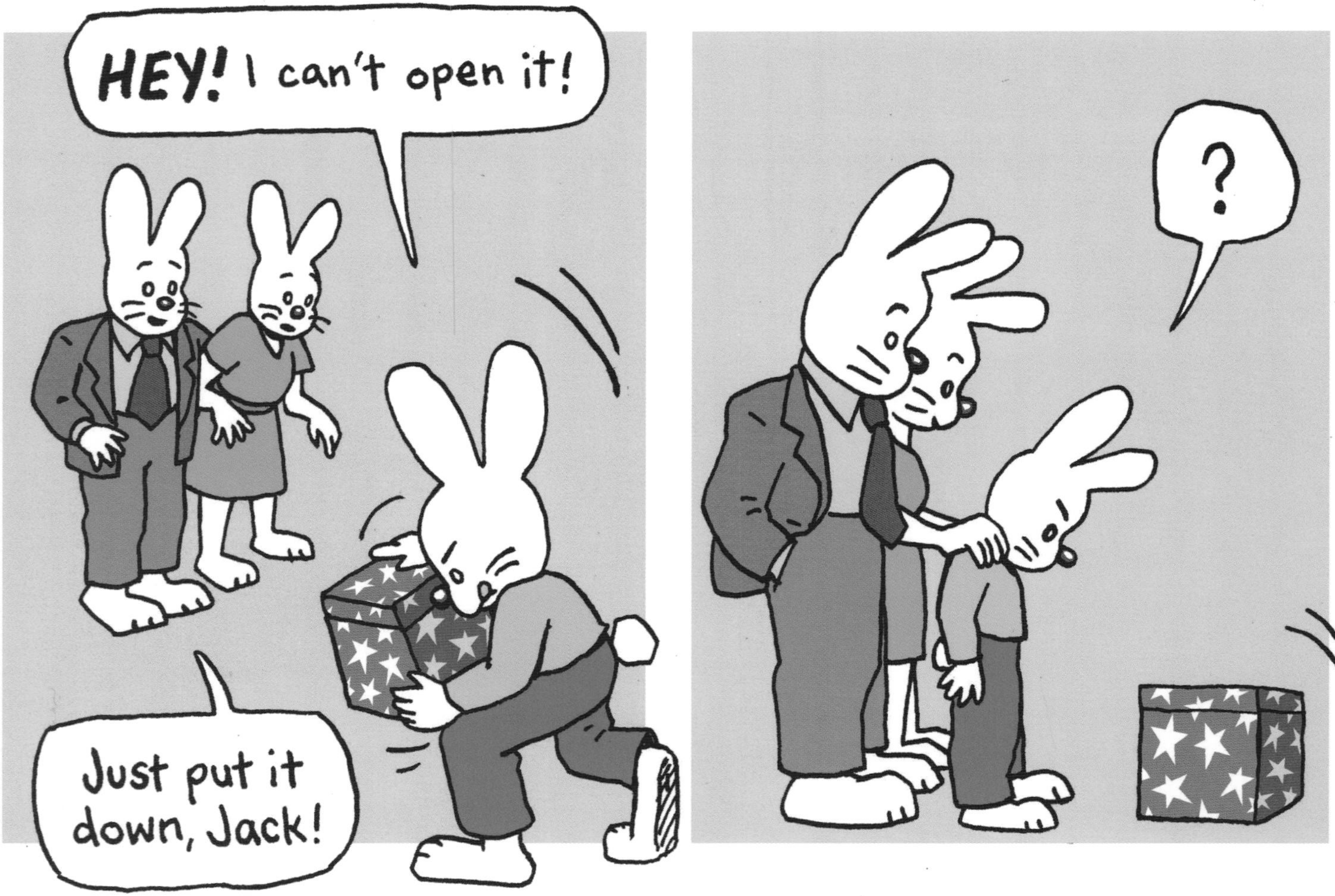
HEY! I can't open it!
Just put it down, Jack!
?

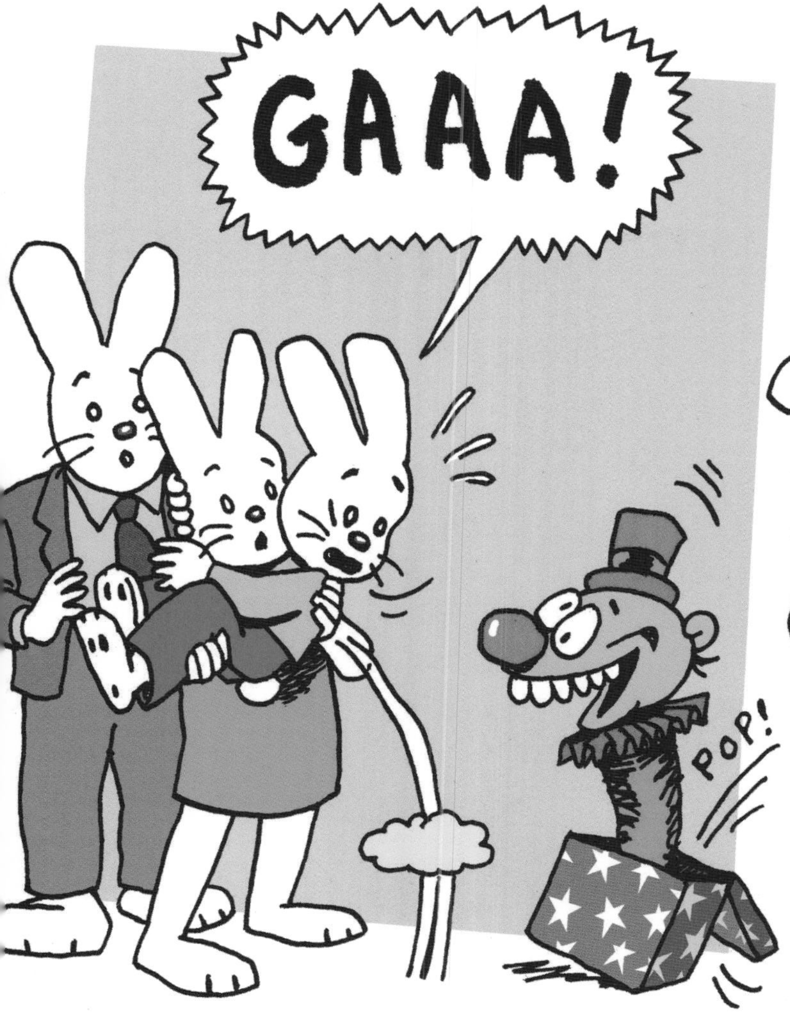
GAAA!
POP!

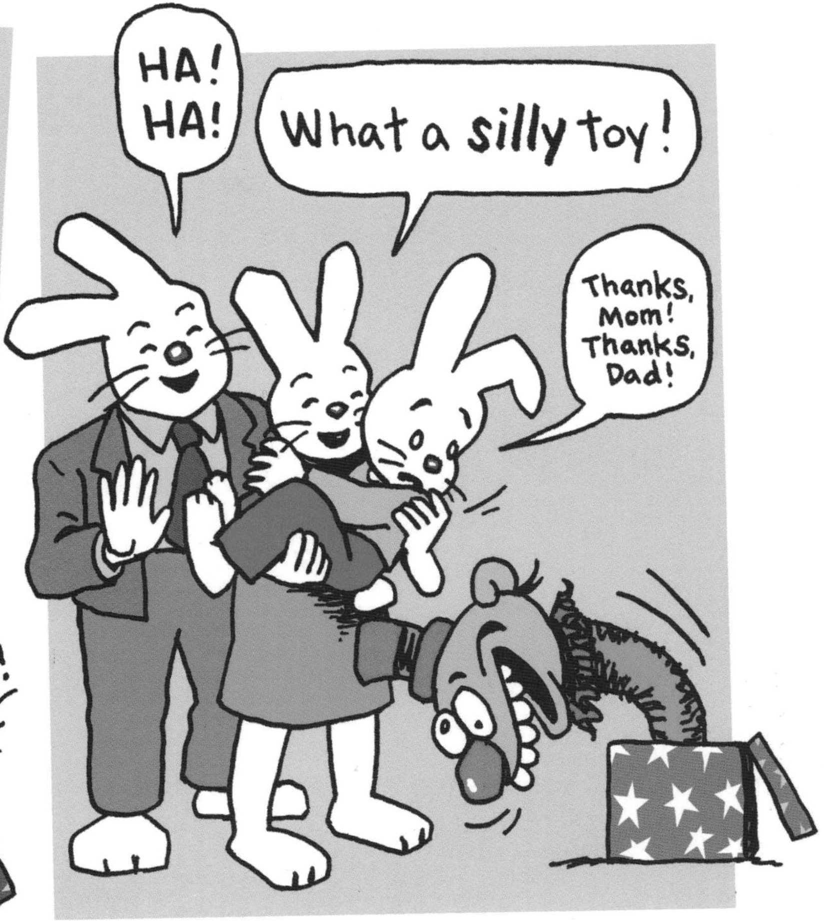
HA! HA!
What a silly toy!
Thanks, Mom! Thanks, Dad!

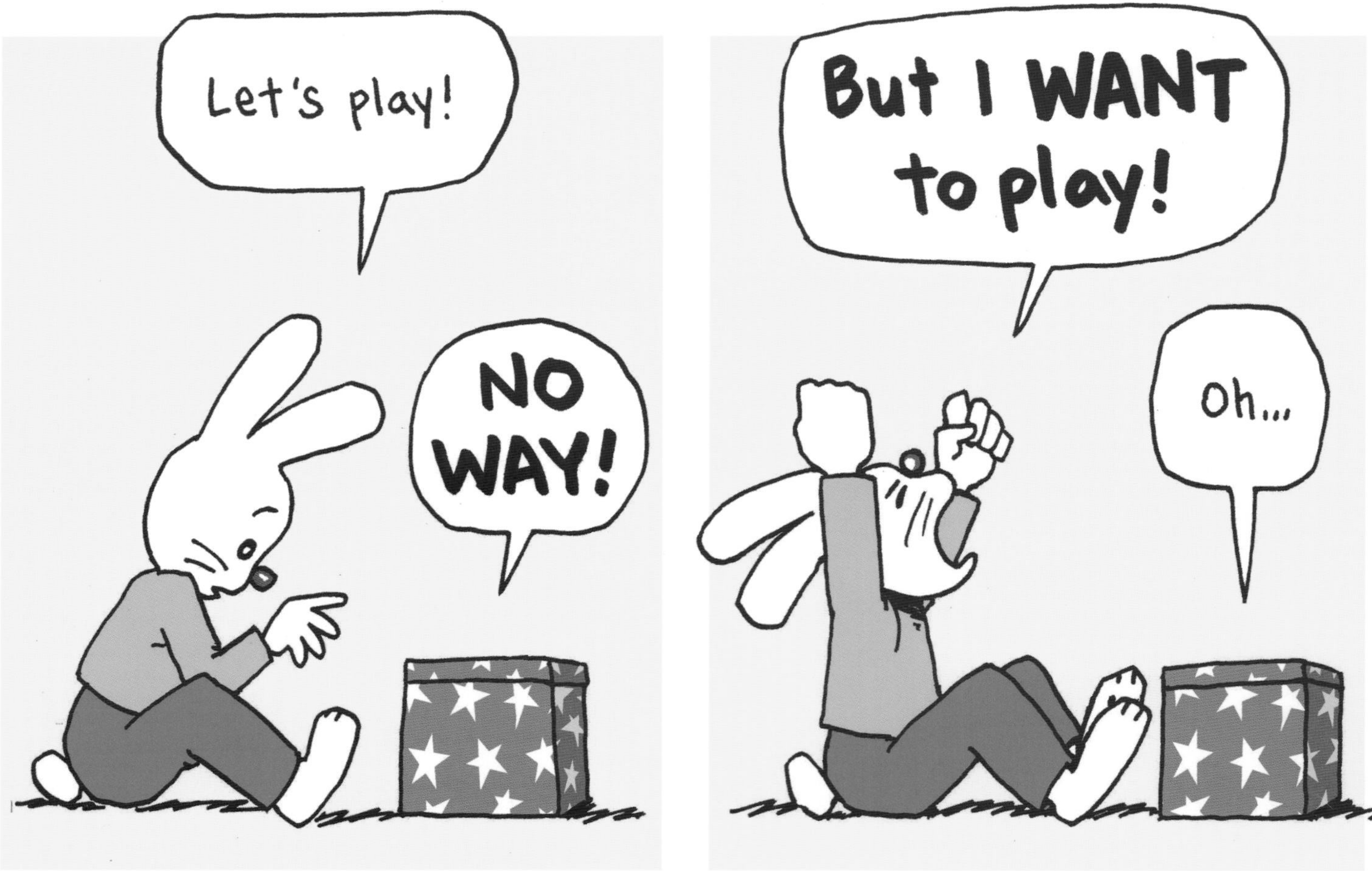
Let's play!
NO WAY!
But I WANT to play!
Oh...

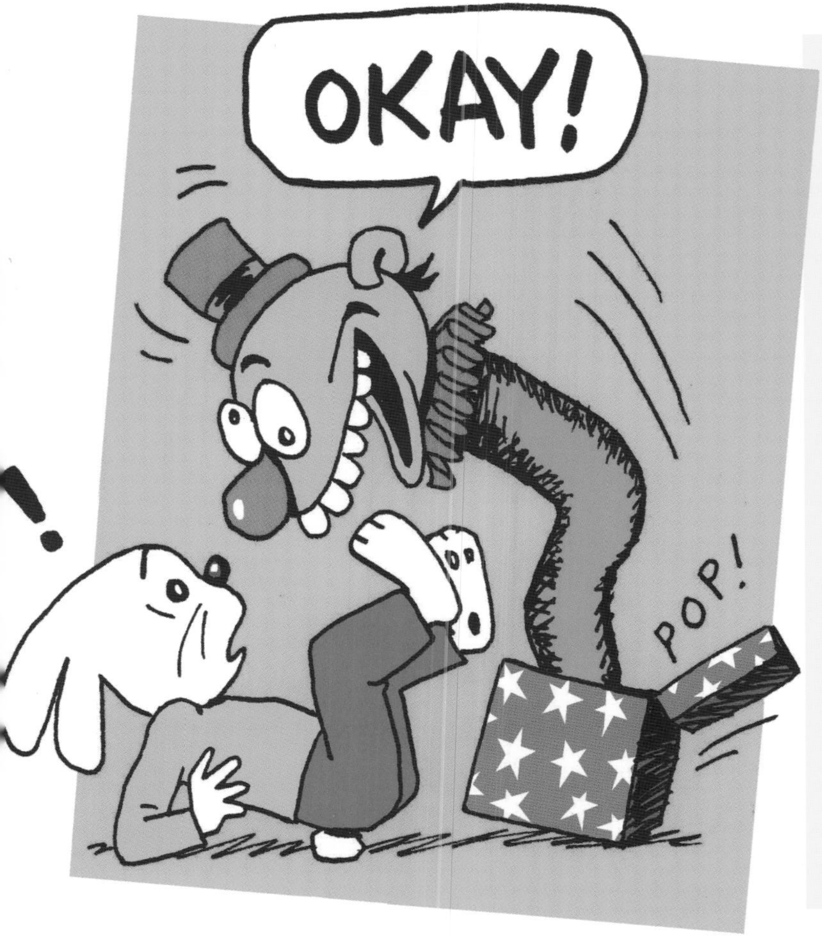
OKAY!
!
POP!

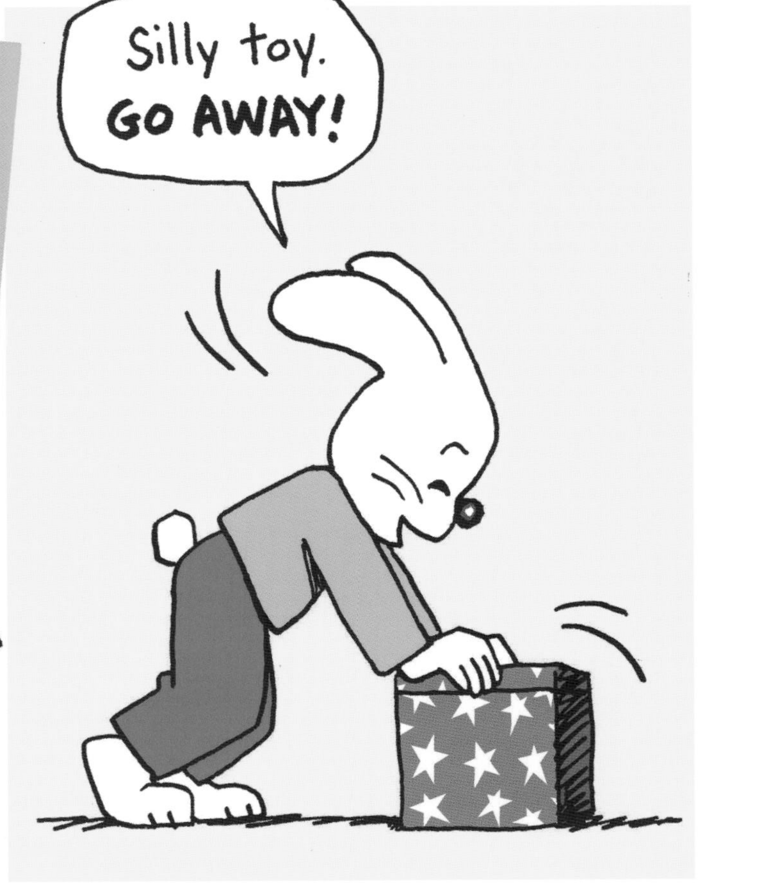
Silly toy.
GO AWAY!

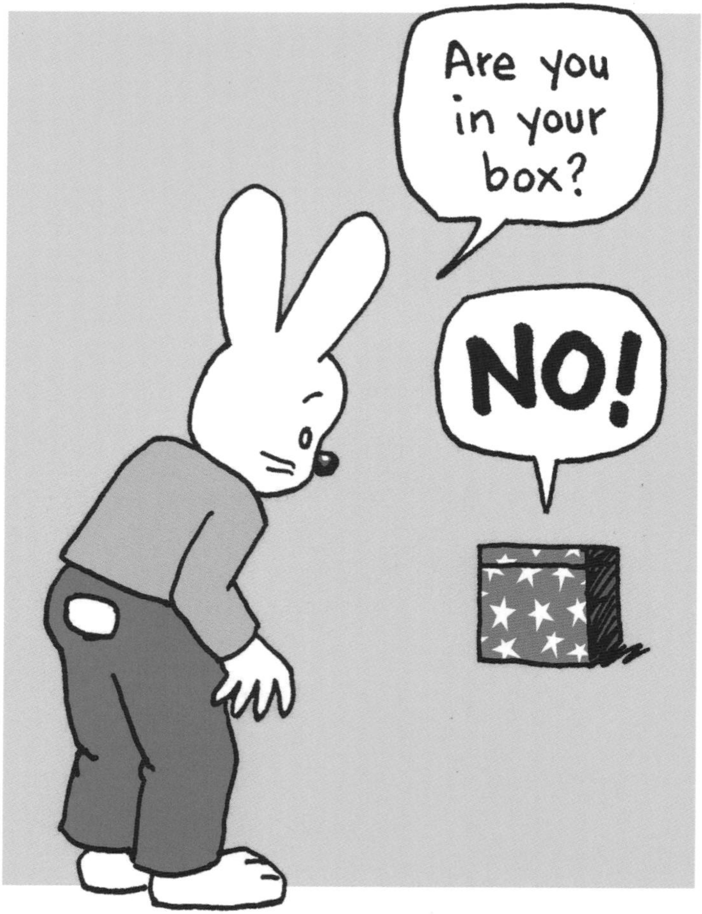
Are you in your box?
NO!

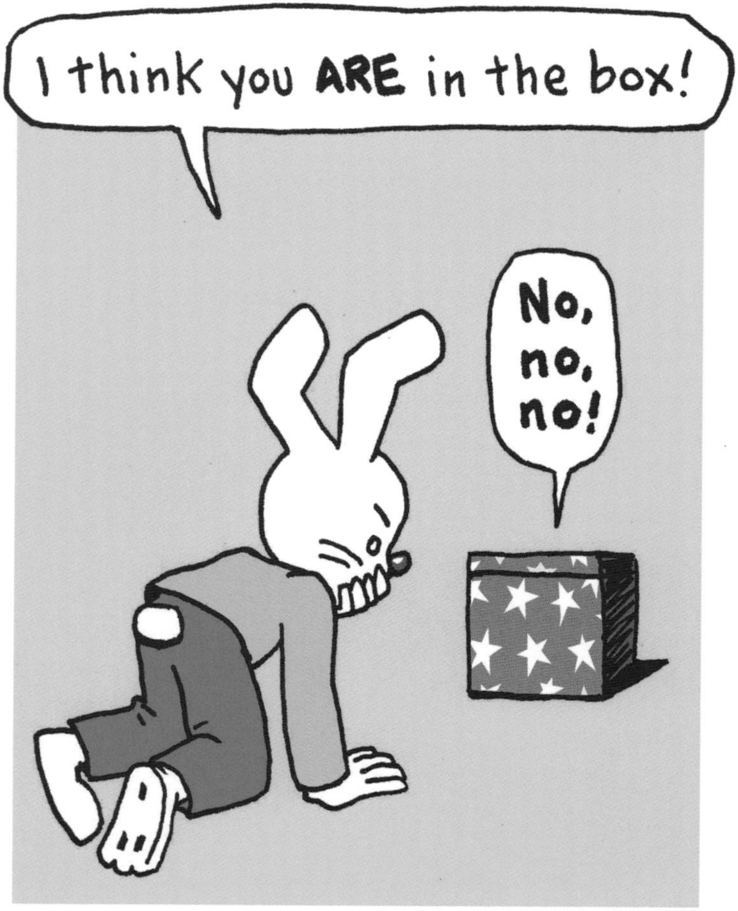
I think you **ARE** in the box!
No, no, no!

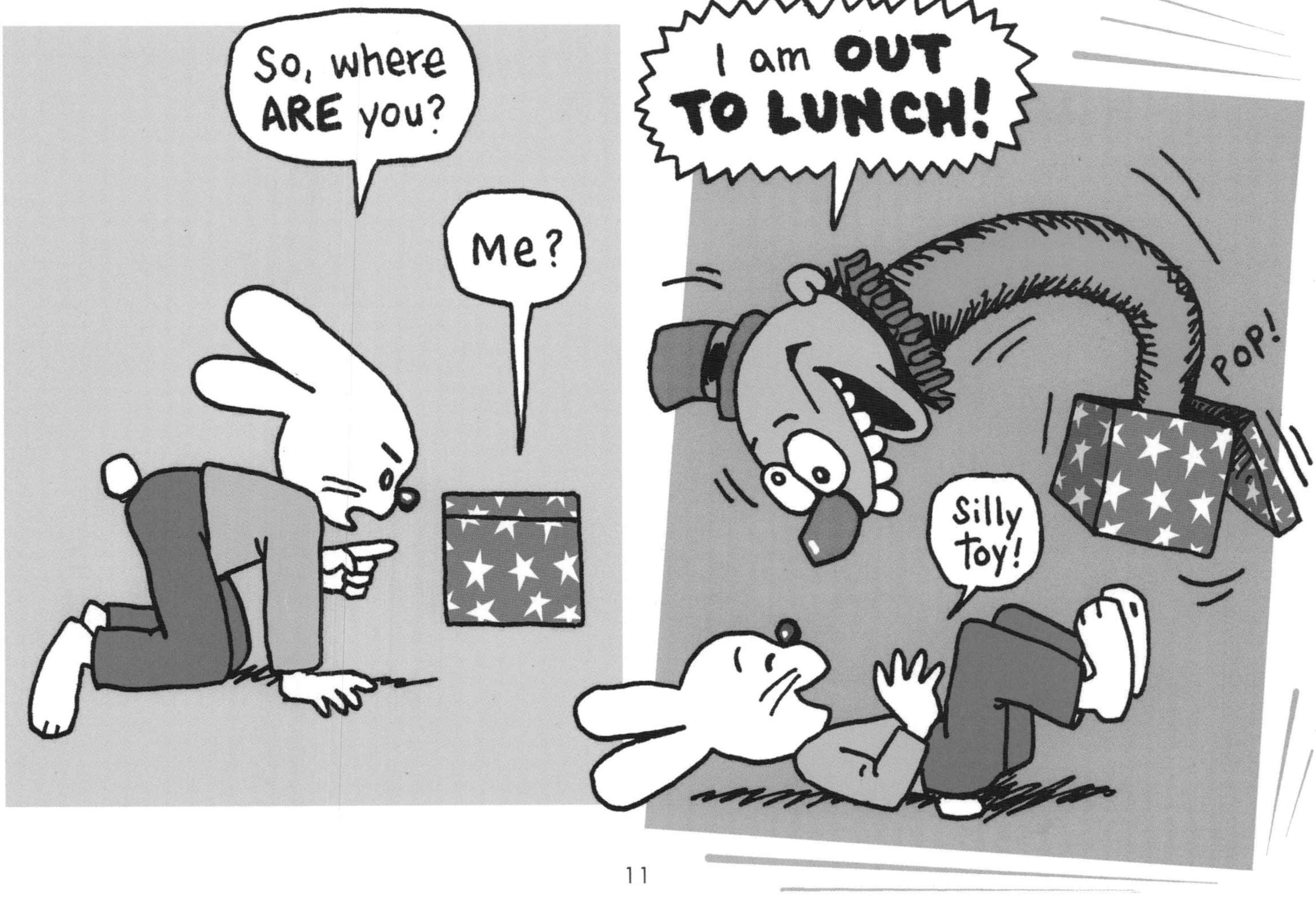
So, where **ARE** you?
Me?
I am **OUT TO LUNCH!**
POP!
Silly toy!

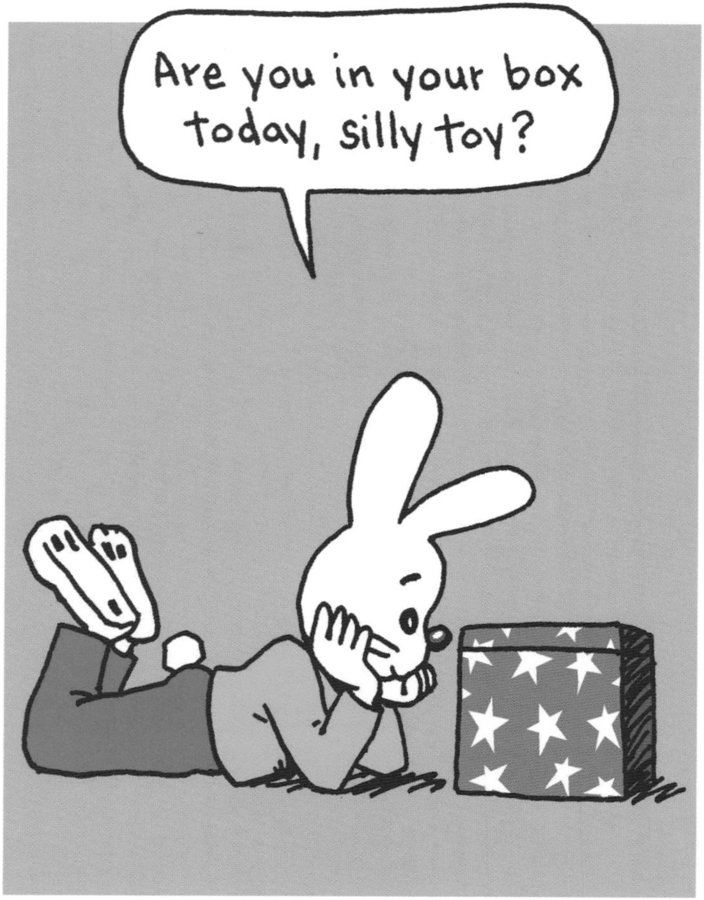
Are you in your box today, silly toy?

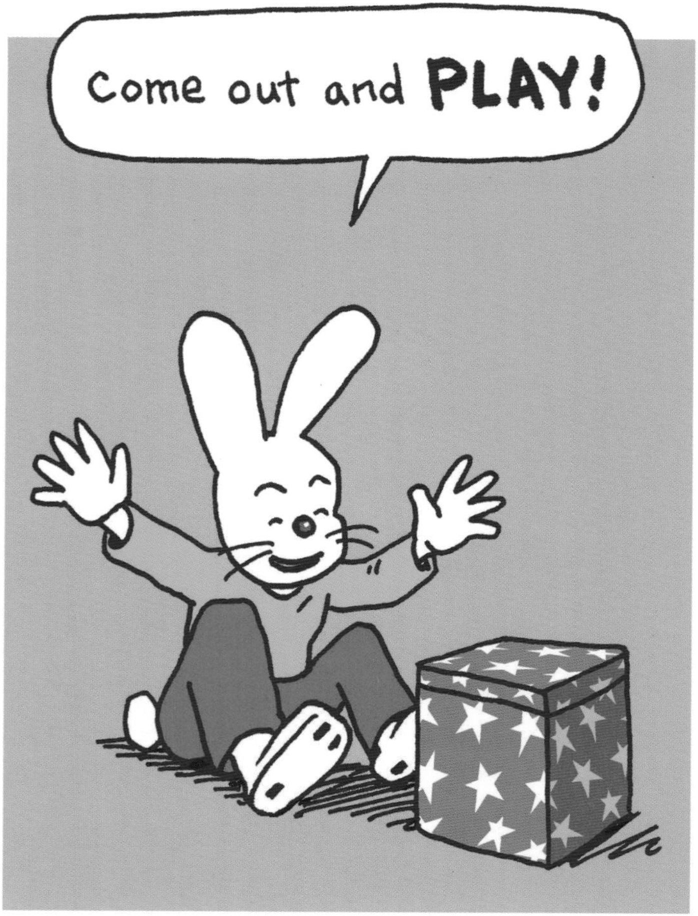
Come out and **PLAY!**

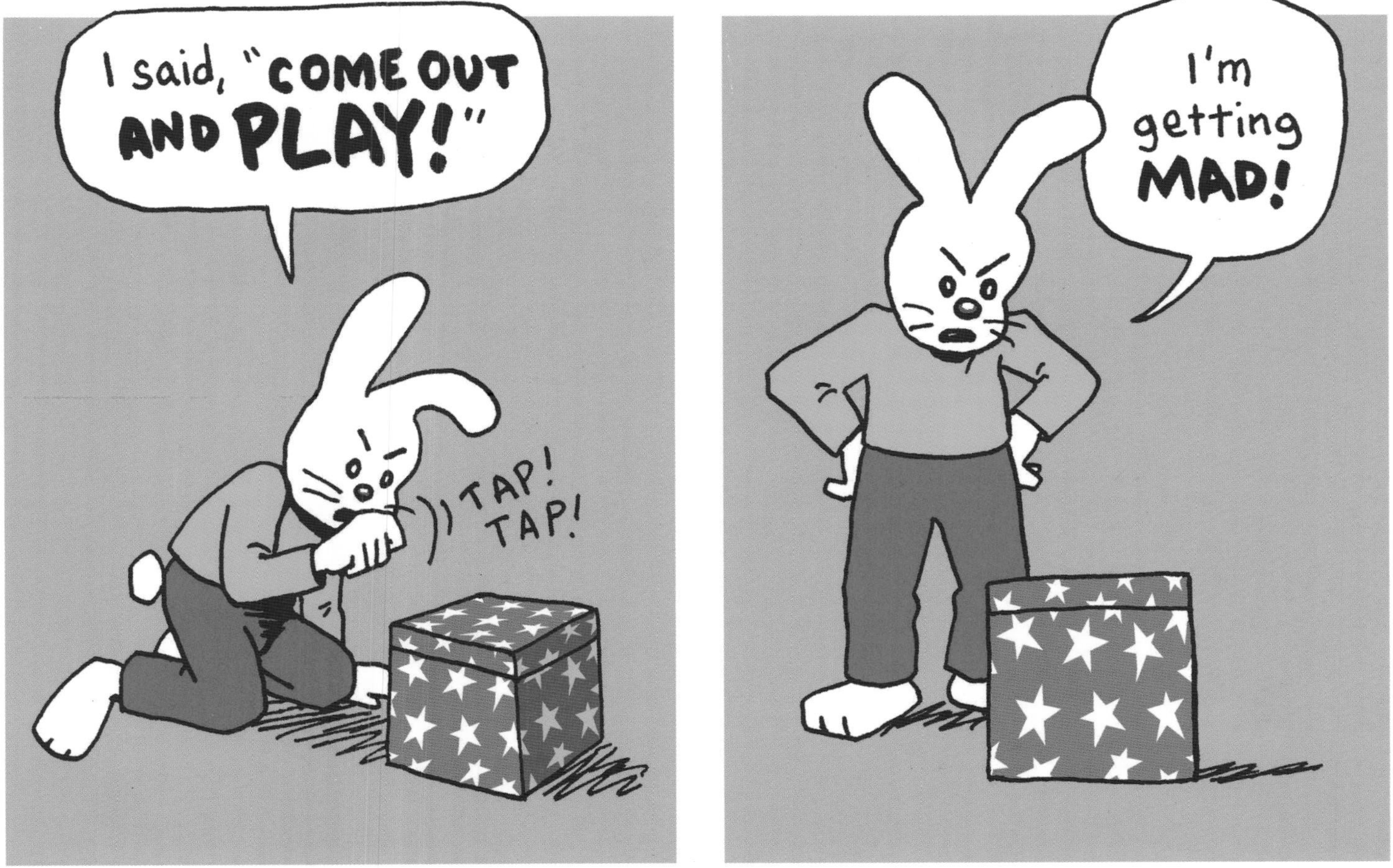
I said, "COME OUT AND PLAY!"
TAP! TAP!
I'm getting MAD!

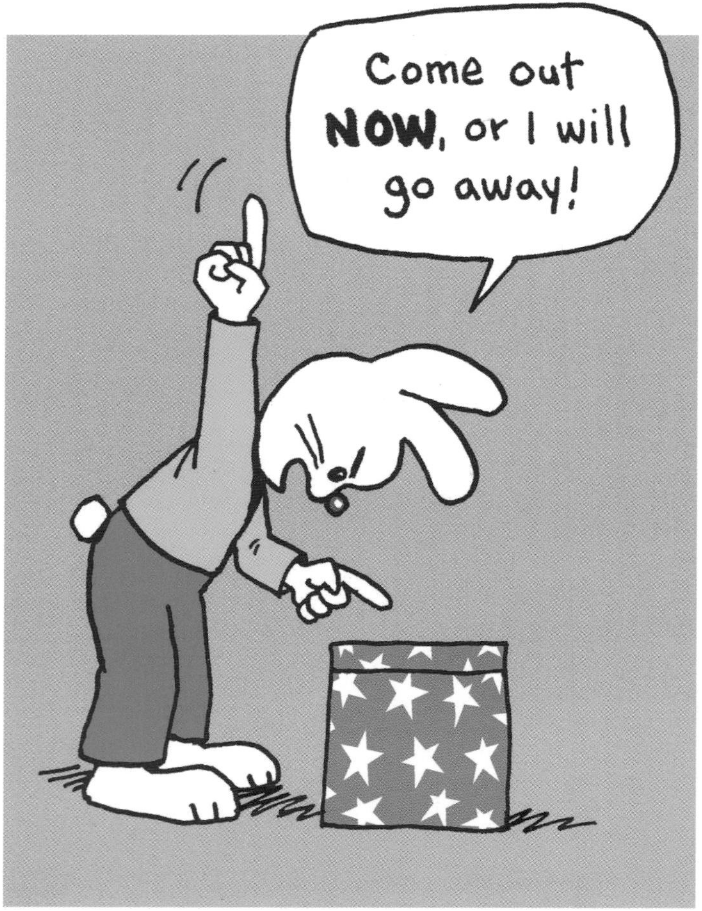
Come out NOW, or I will go away!

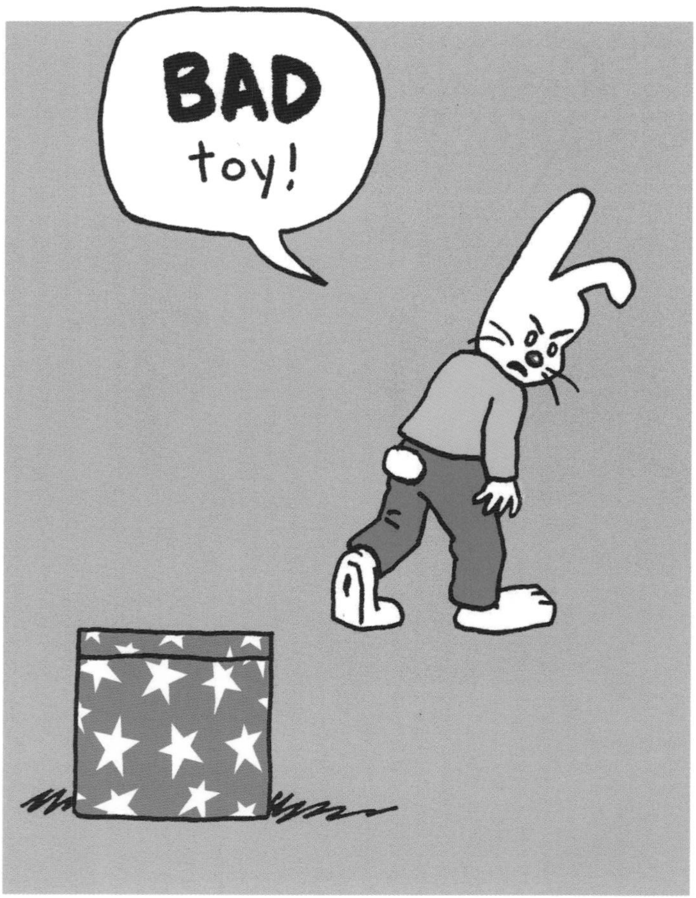
BAD toy!

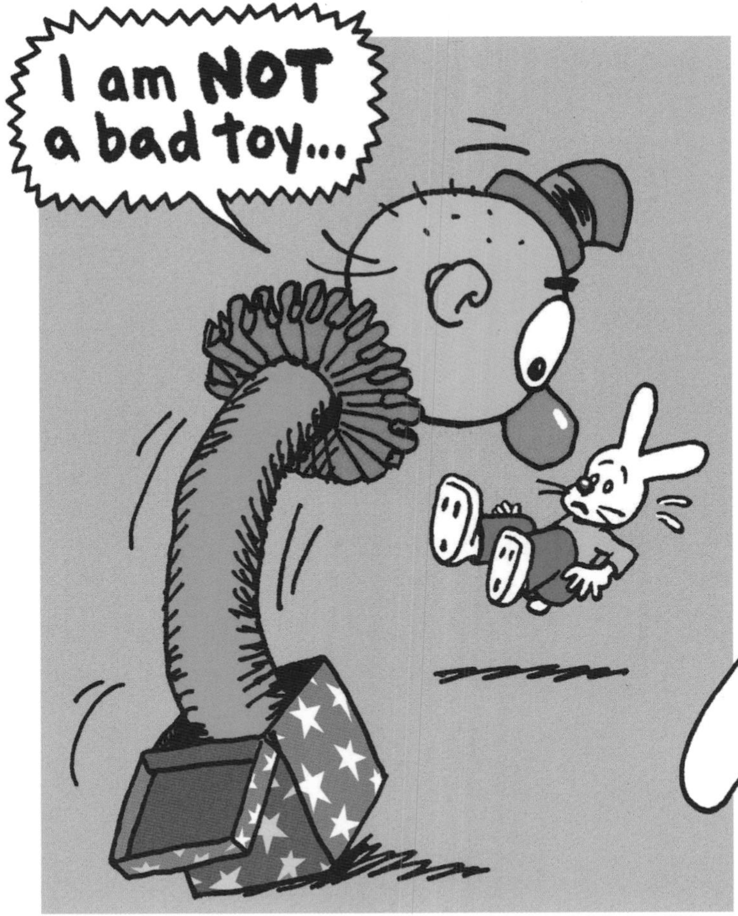
I am NOT a bad toy...

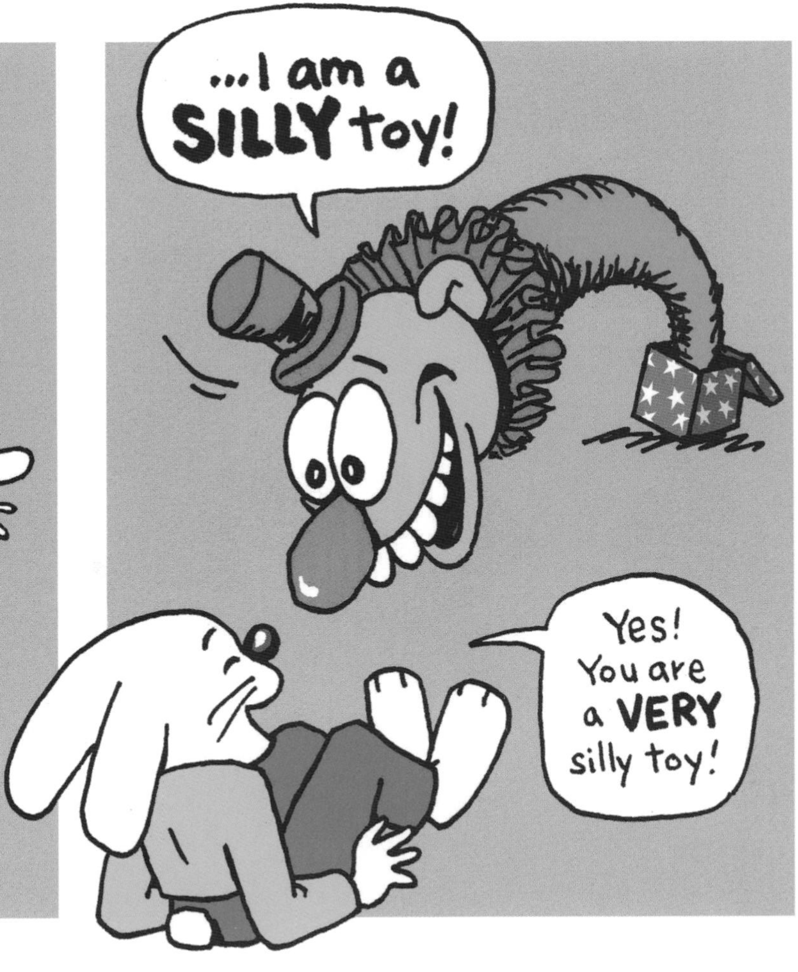
...I am a SILLY toy!
Yes! You are a VERY silly toy!

Hi, Silly Toy. How are you today?
BAH!
My name is **NOT** Silly Toy!
Well, what **IS** your name?

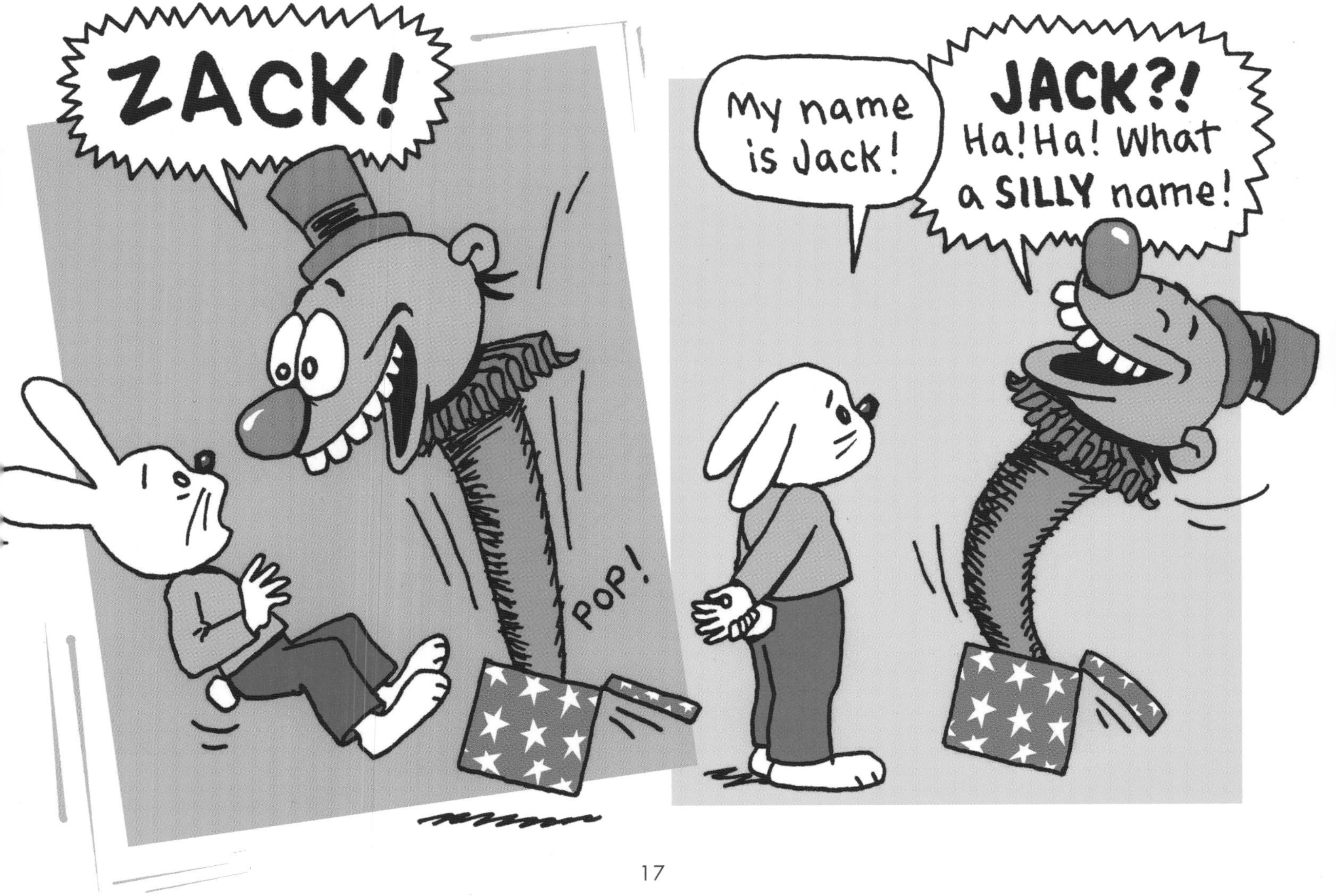
ZACK!
POP!
My name is Jack!
JACK?! Ha! Ha! What a SILLY name!

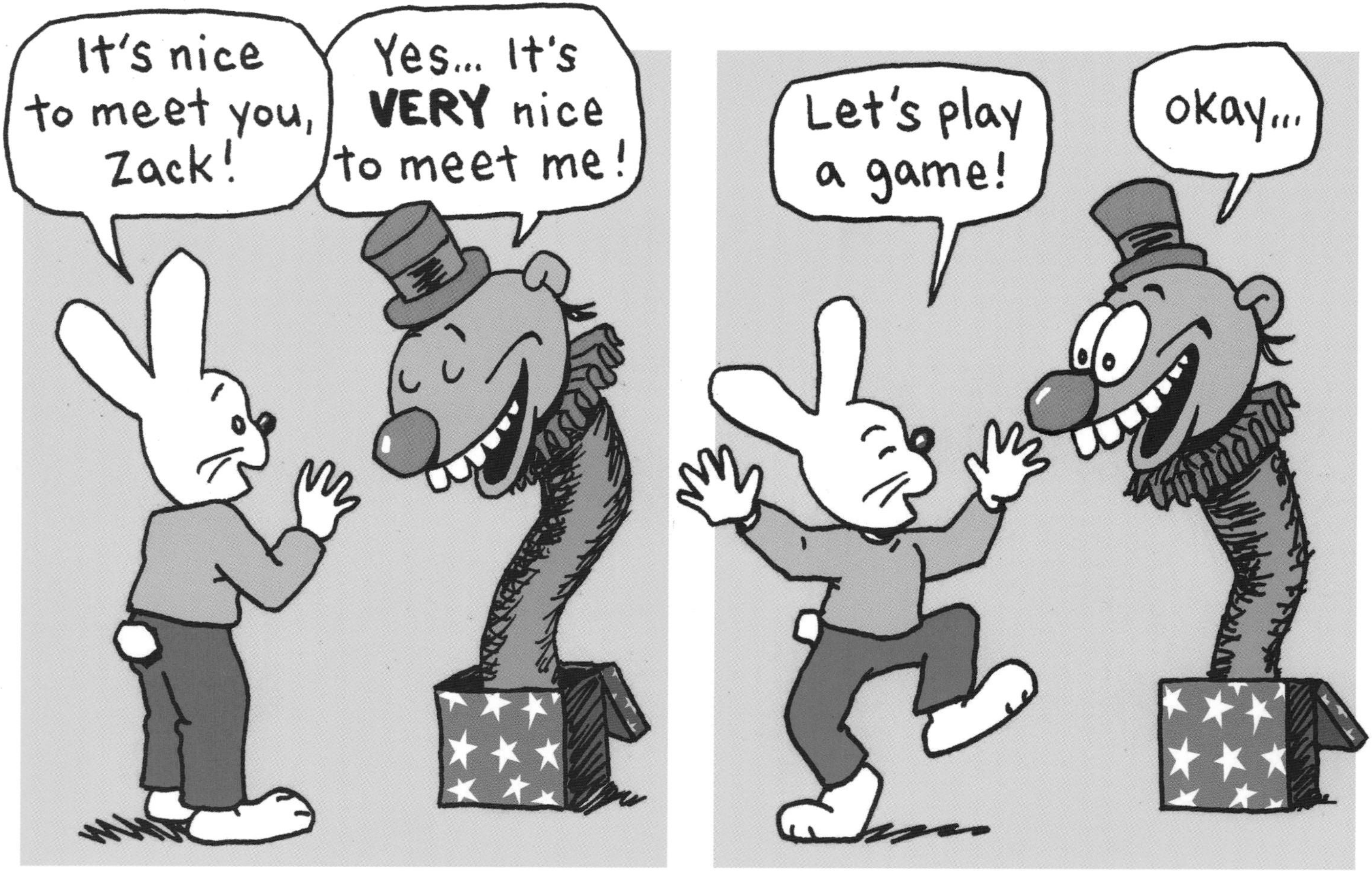
It's nice to meet you, Zack!
Yes... It's **VERY** nice to meet me!
Let's play a game!
Okay...

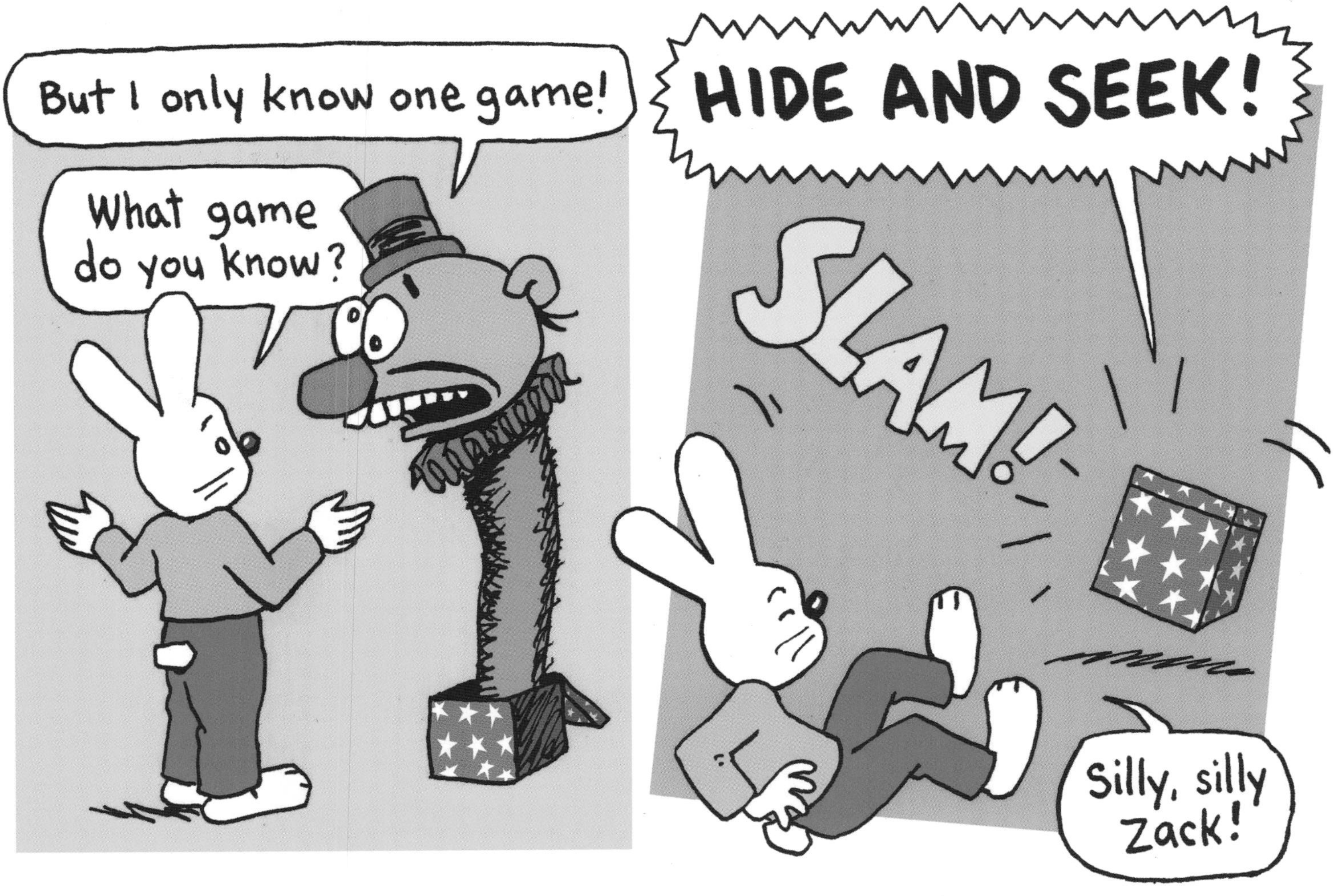
But I only know one game!
What game do you know?
HIDE AND SEEK!
SLAM!
Silly, silly Zack!

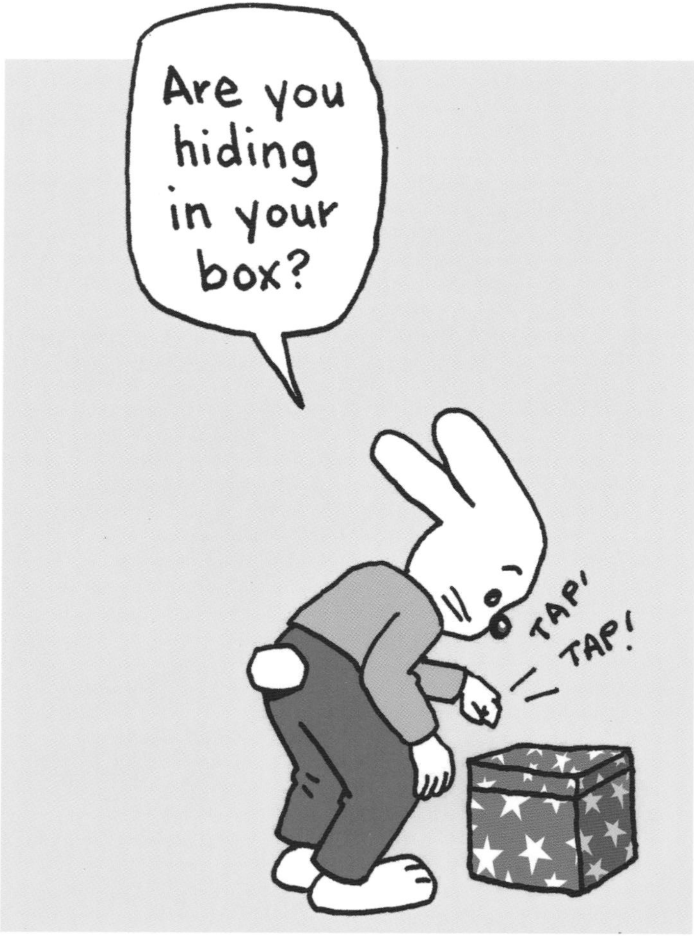
Are you hiding in your box?
TAP! TAP!

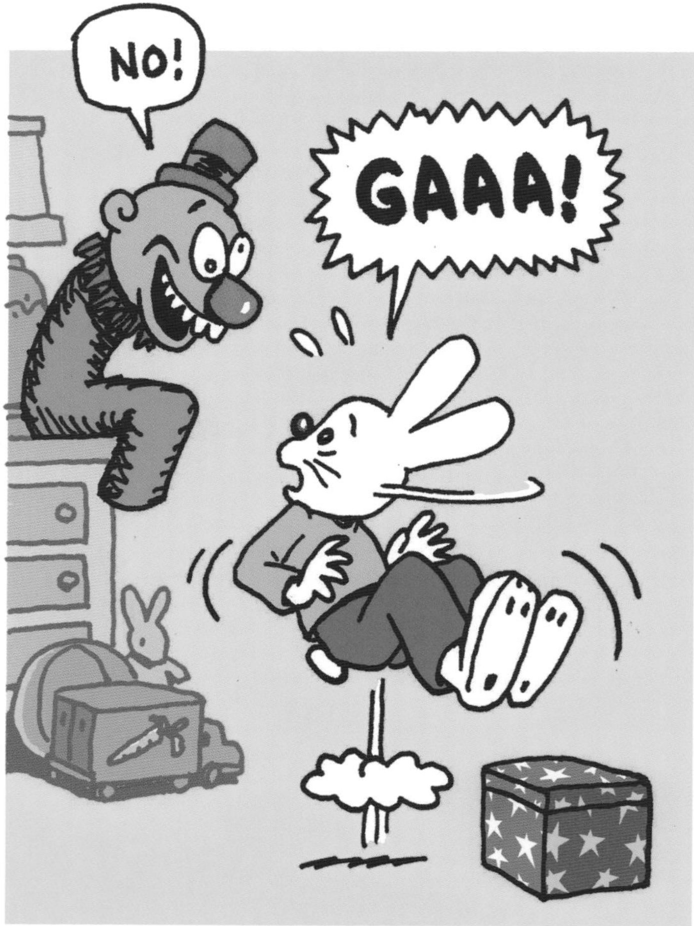
NO!
GAAA!

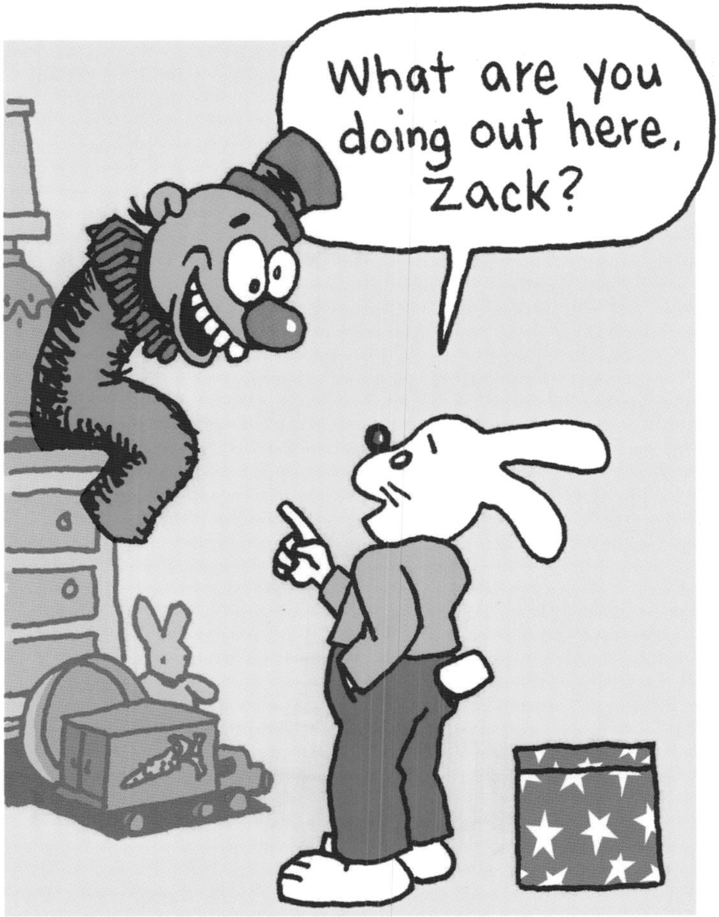
What are you doing out here, Zack?

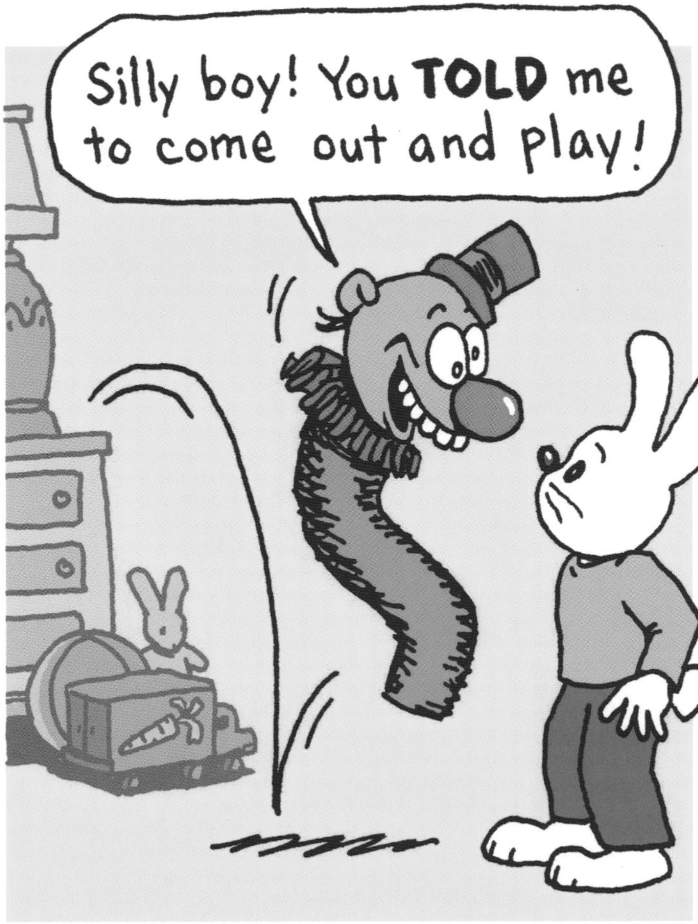
Silly boy! You TOLD me to come out and play!

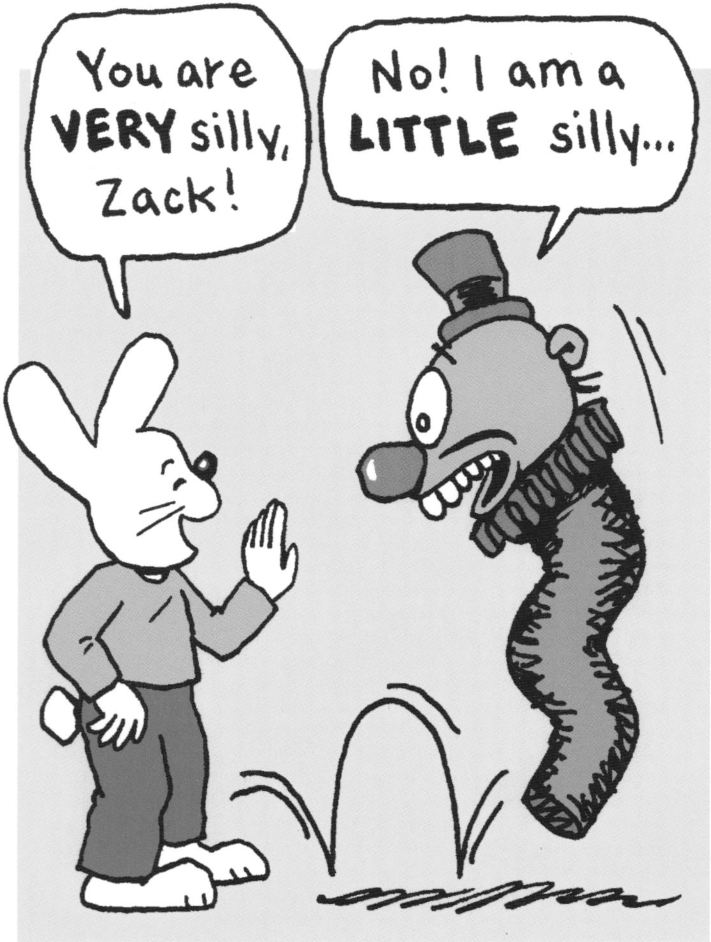
You are VERY silly, Zack!
No! I am a LITTLE silly...

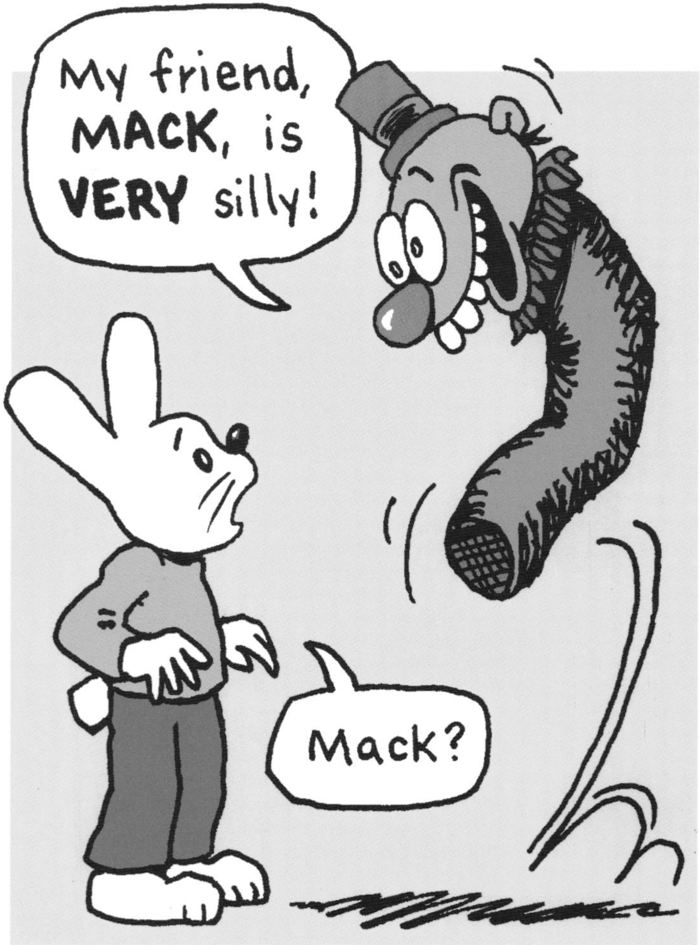
My friend, MACK, is VERY silly!
Mack?

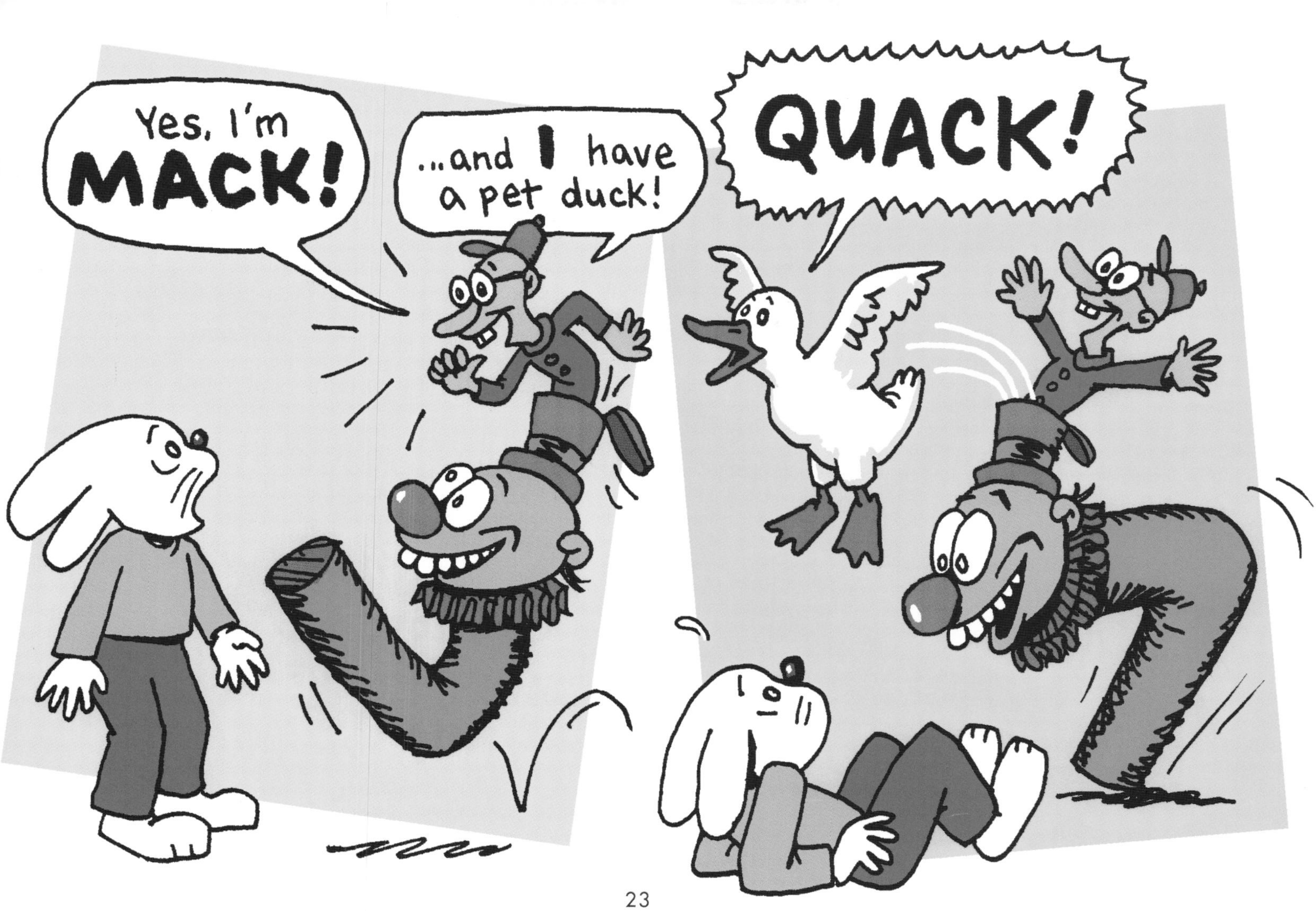

Yes, I'm MACK!
...and I have a pet duck!
QUACK!

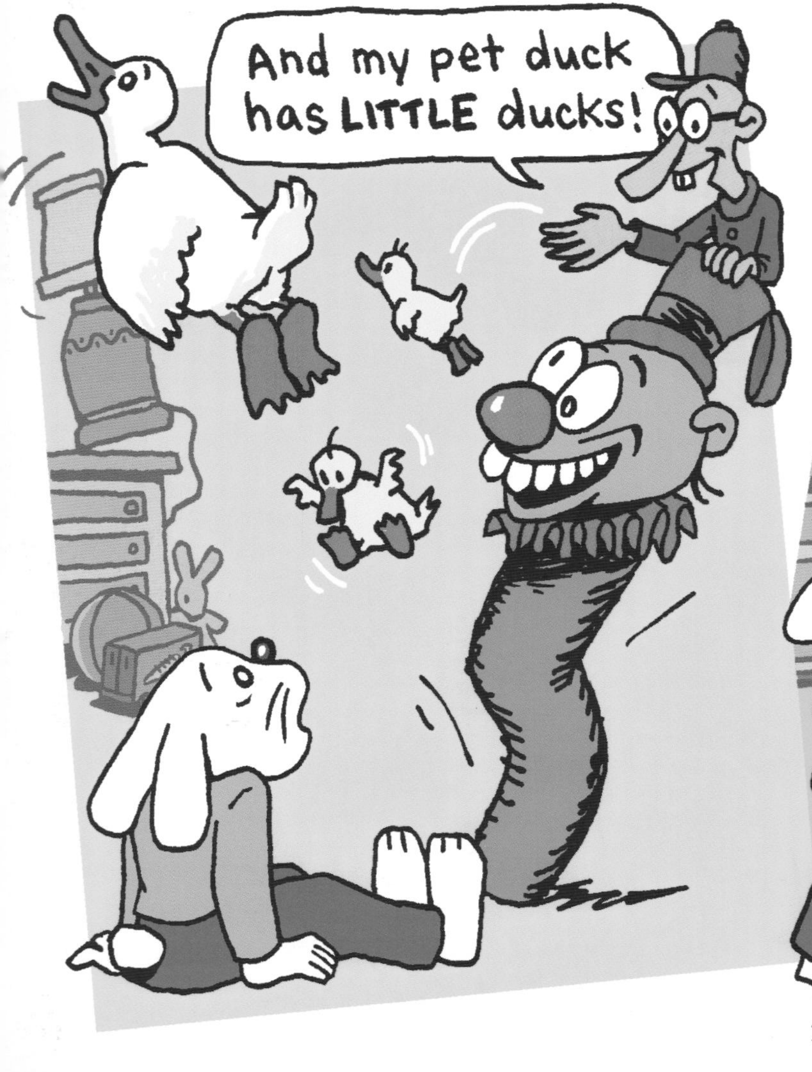
And my pet duck has LITTLE ducks!

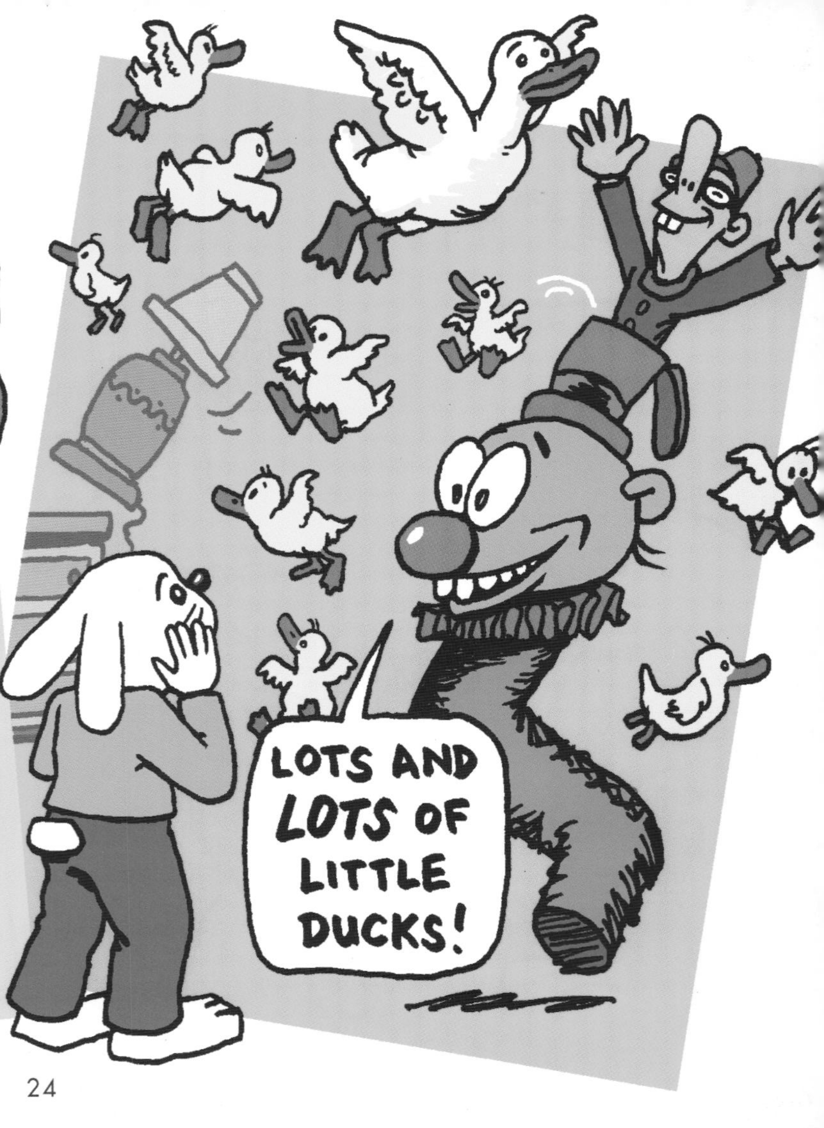
LOTS AND LOTS OF LITTLE DUCKS!

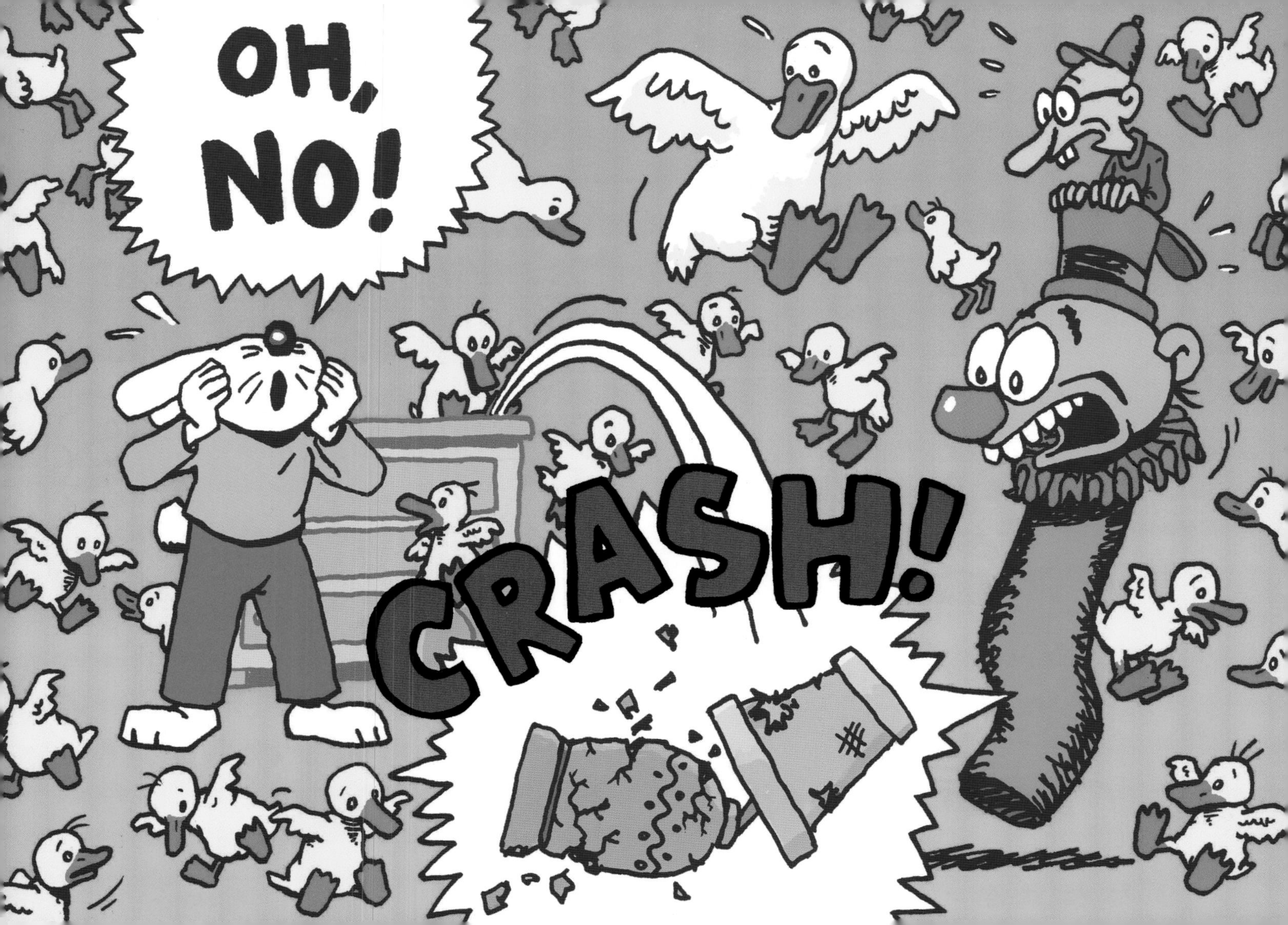
OH, NO!
CRASH!

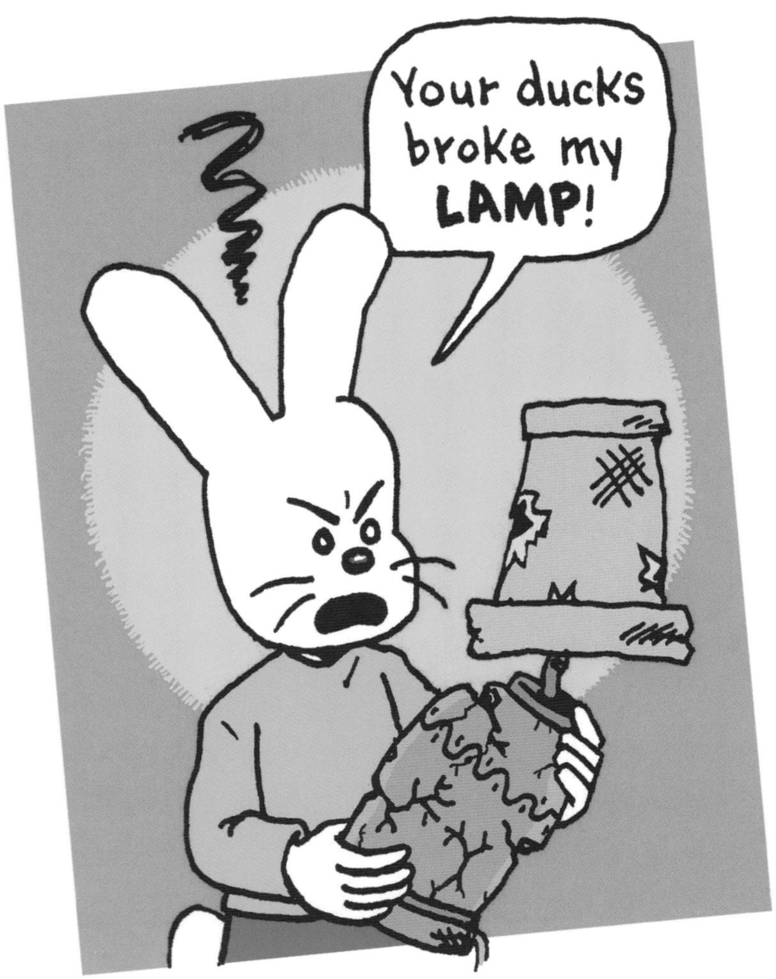
Your ducks broke my **LAMP**!

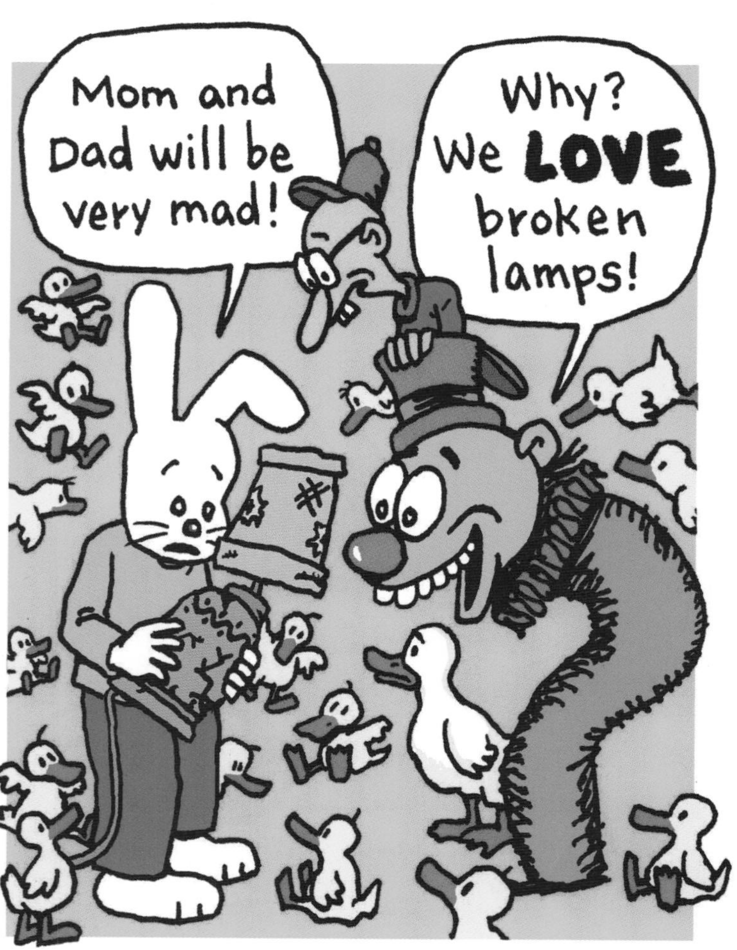
Mom and Dad will be very mad!
Why? We **LOVE** broken lamps!

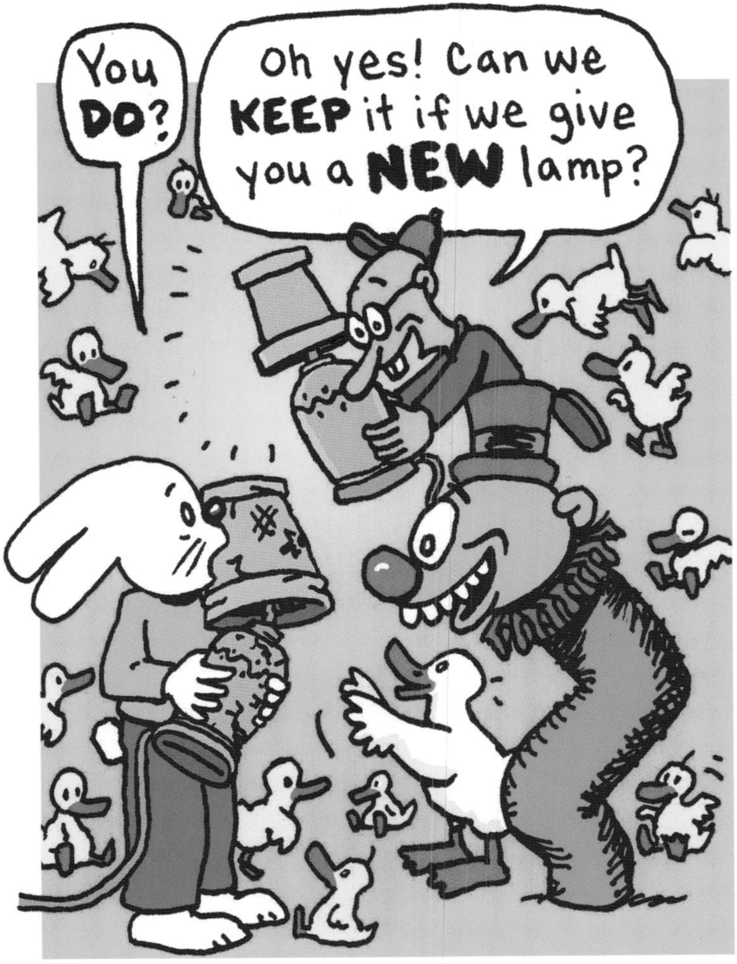
You DO?
Oh yes! Can we KEEP it if we give you a NEW lamp?

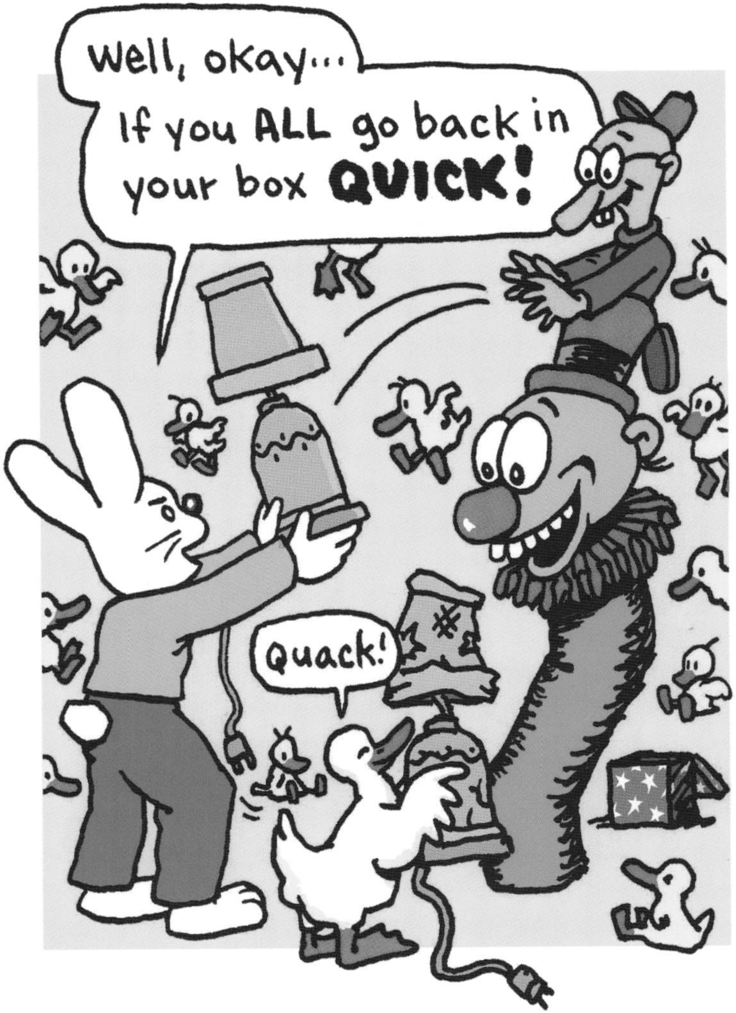
Well, okay... If you ALL go back in your box QUICK!
Quack!

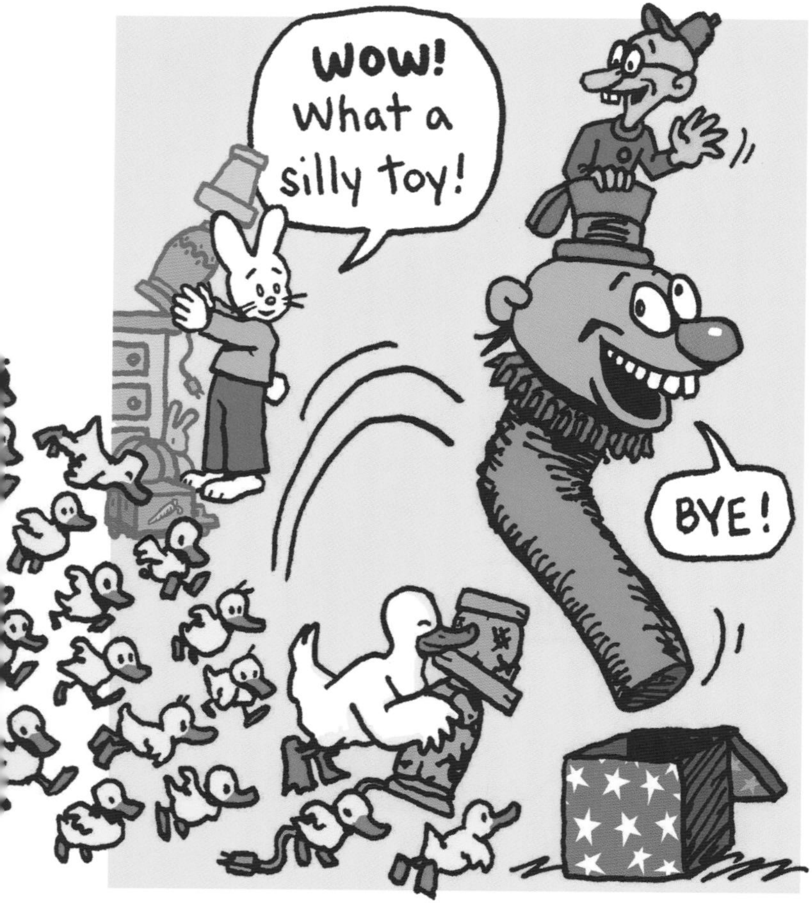
WOW! What a silly toy!
BYE!

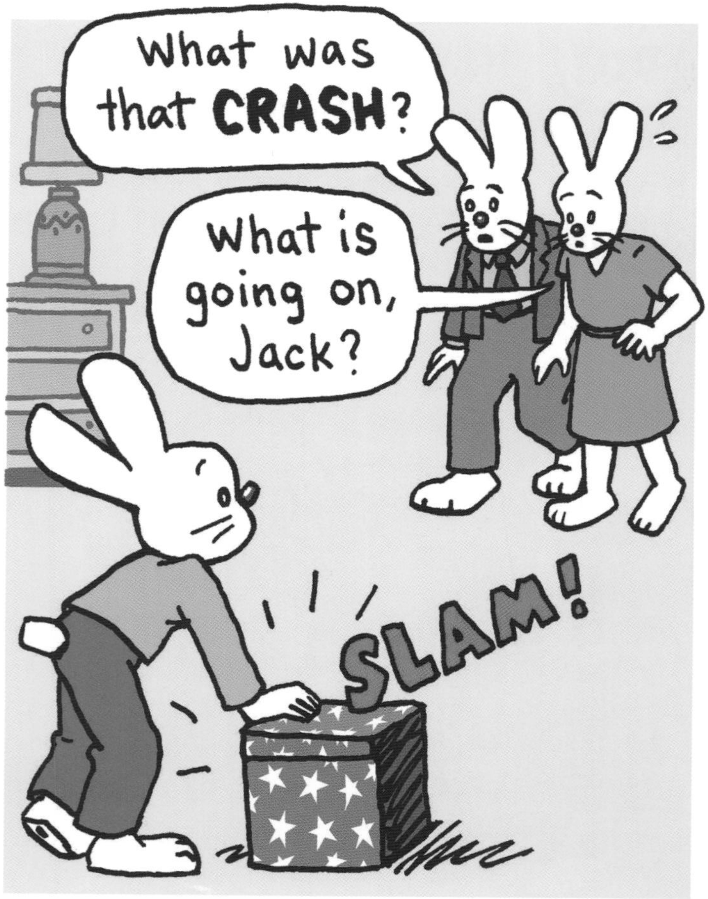
What was that CRASH?
What is going on, Jack?
SLAM!

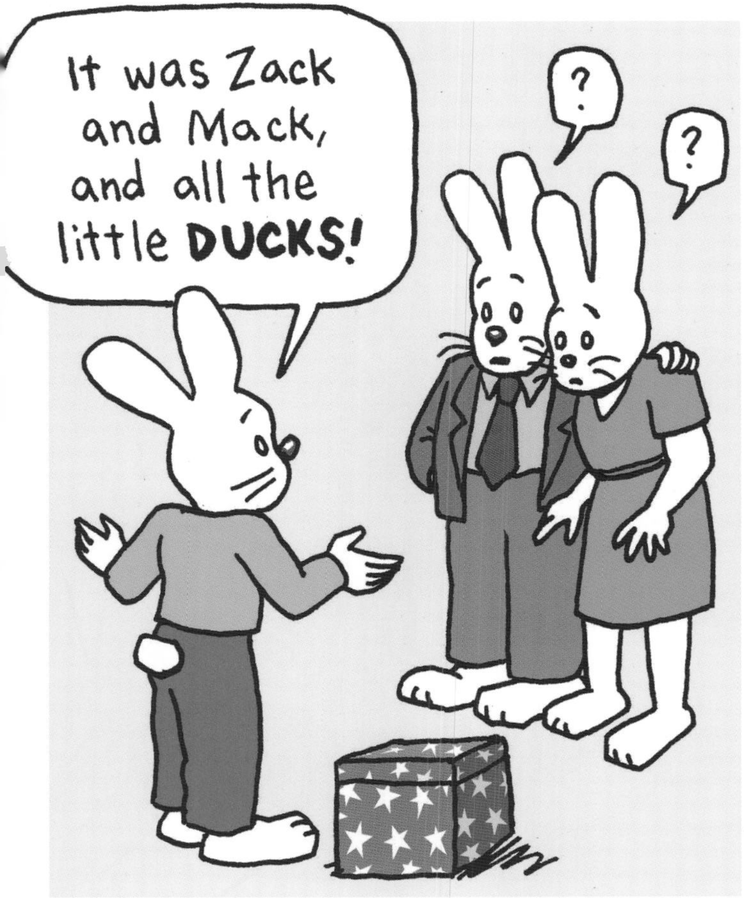
It was Zack and Mack, and all the little **DUCKS!**
?
?

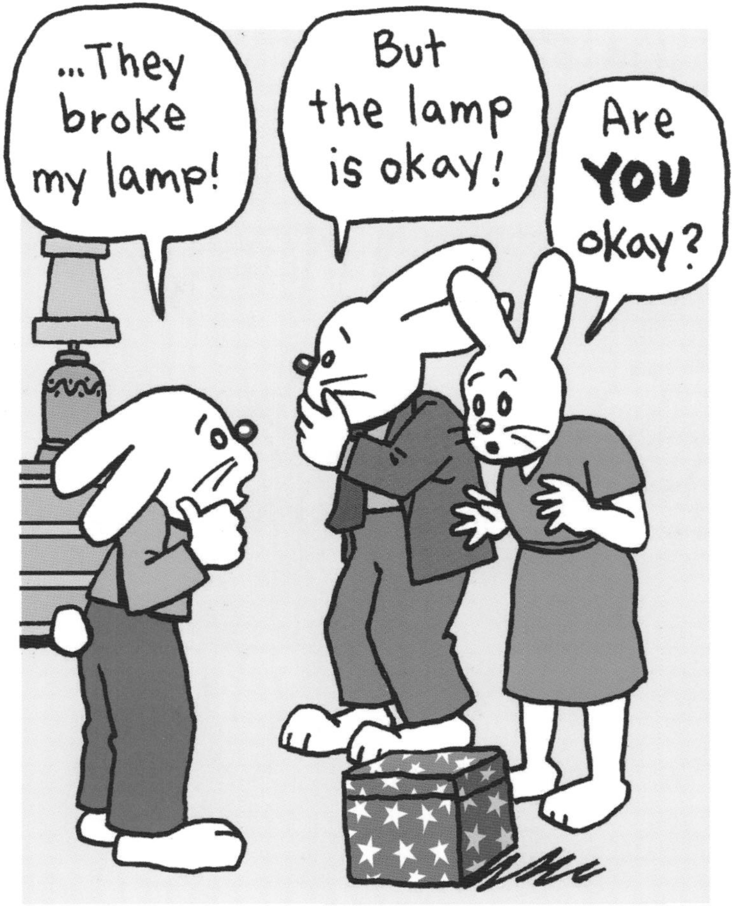
...They broke my lamp!
But the lamp is okay!
Are **YOU** okay?

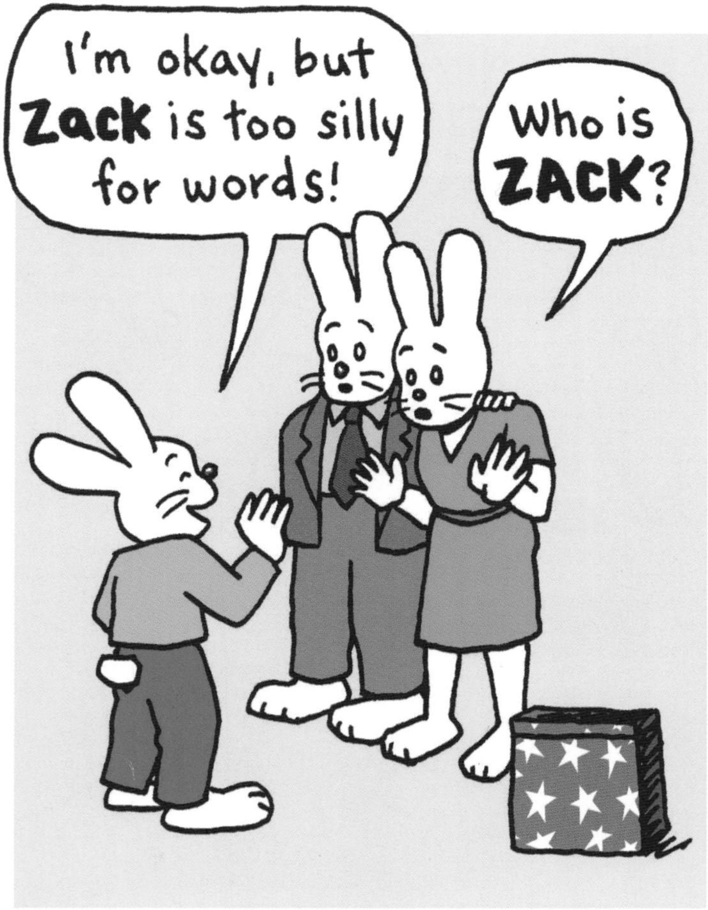
I'm okay, but ZACK is too silly for words!
Who is ZACK?

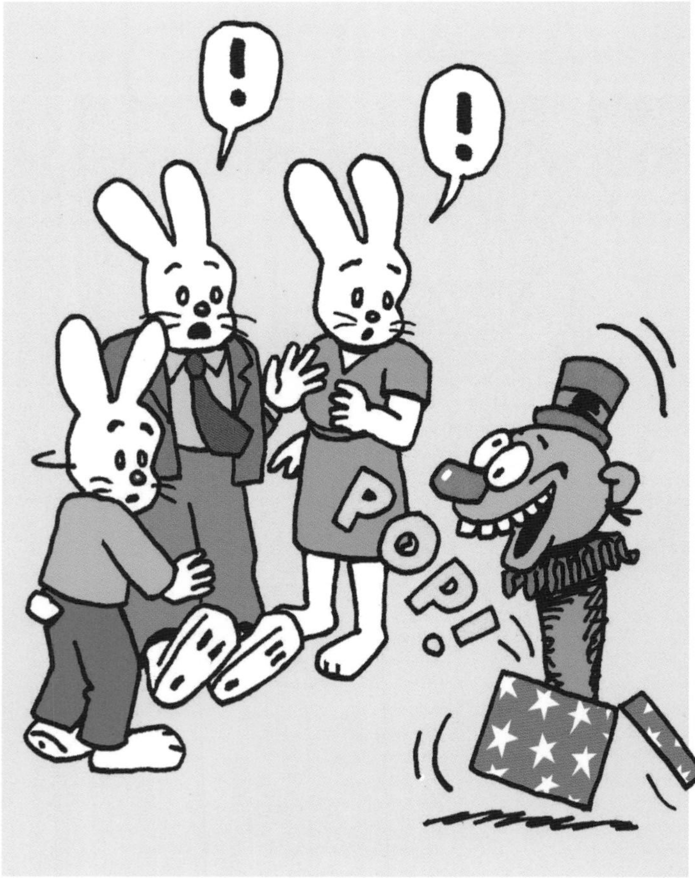
!
!
POP!

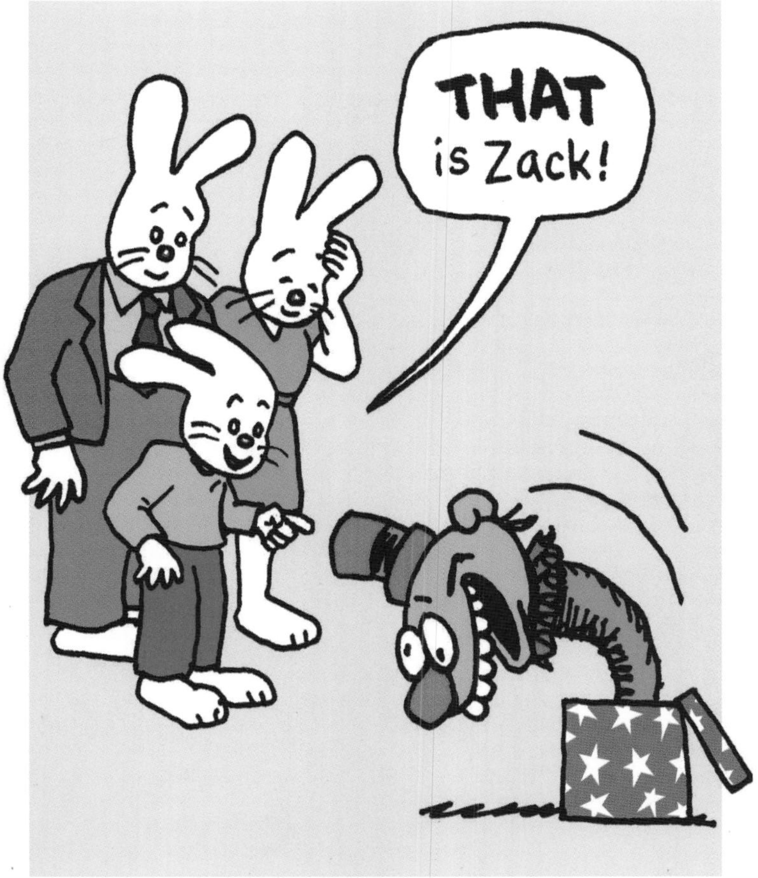
THAT
is Zack!

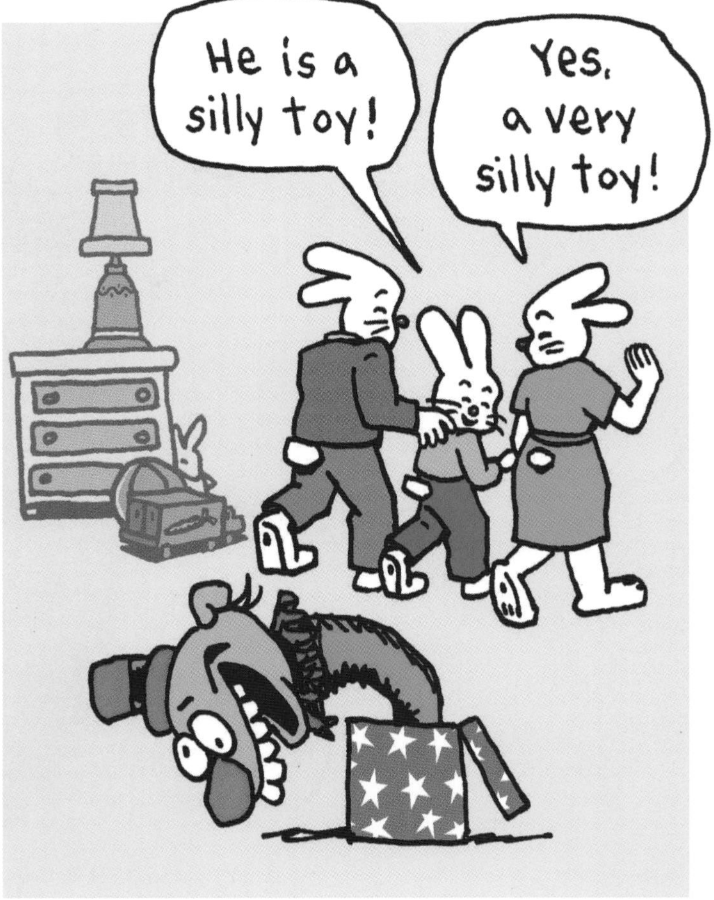
He is a
silly toy!
Yes.
a very
silly toy!

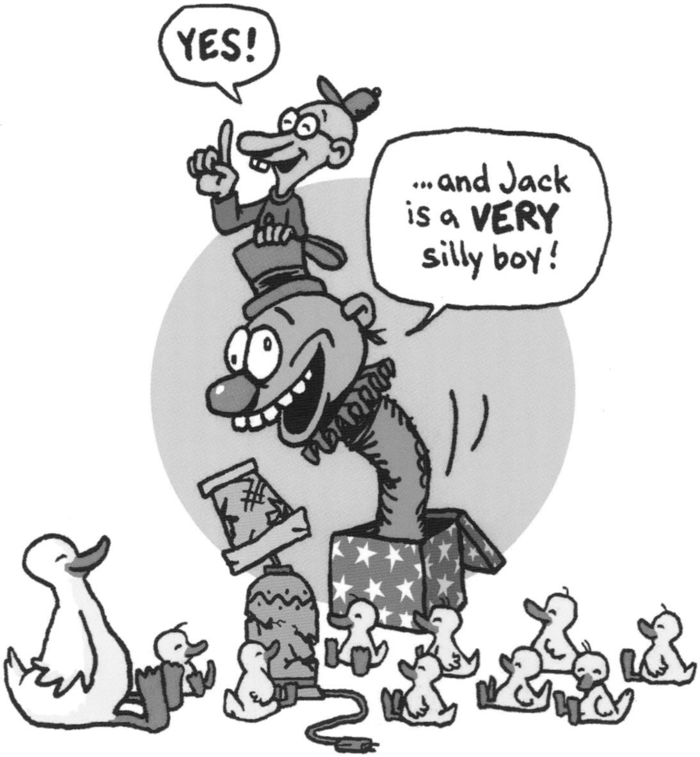
YES!
...and Jack is a **VERY** silly boy!

ABOUT THE AUTHOR

ART SPIEGELMAN learned to read from looking at comics, "trying to find out if Batman was a Good Guy or a Bad Guy." His now very grownup kids, Nadja and Dash, learned to read from comics, too. He says, "I sacrificed a very valuable collection of old comic books to fatherhood."

He is the author of the Pulitzer Prize winning *MAUS: A Survivor's Tale.* His most recent book for grownups is *MetaMaus.* His work for children includes the best-selling *Open Me... I'm a Dog!* and the *Little Lit* series of comics anthologies, for which he was both co-editor and contributor. He and his wife, Françoise Mouly, live in New York City. Their cat, Houdini, never learned to read.

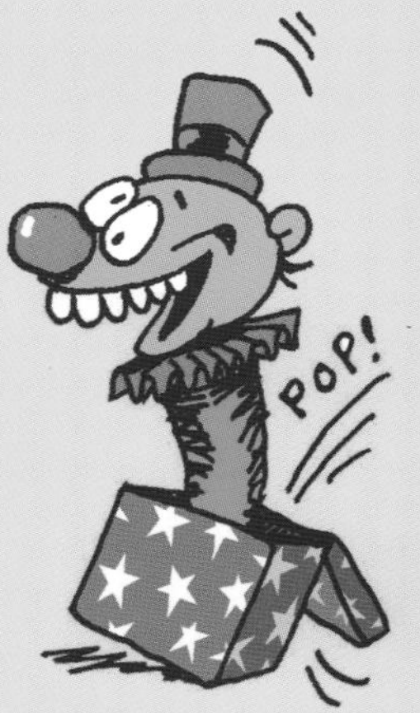
POP!

TIPS FOR PARENTS AND TEACHERS:

HOW TO READ COMICS WITH KIDS

Kids love comics! They are naturally drawn to the details in the pictures, which make them want to read the words. Comics beg for repeated readings and let both emerging and reluctant readers enjoy complex stories with a rich vocabulary. But since comics have their own grammar, here are a few tips for reading them with kids:

GUIDE YOUNG READERS: Use your finger to show your place in the text, but keep it at the bottom of the speaking character so it doesn't hide the very important facial expressions.

HAM IT UP! Think of the comic book story as a play and don't hesitate to read with expression and intonation. Assign parts or get kids to supply the sound effects, a great way to reinforce phonics skills.

LET THEM GUESS. Comics provide lots of context for the words, so emerging readers can make informed guesses. Like jigsaw puzzles, comics ask readers to make connections, so check a young audience's understanding by asking "What's this character thinking?" (but don't be surprised if a kid finds some of the comics' subtle details faster than you).

TALK ABOUT THE PICTURES. Point out how the artist paces the story with pauses (silent panels) or speeded-up action (a burst of short panels). Discuss how the size and shape of the panels carry meaning.

ABOVE ALL, ENJOY! There is of course never one right way to read, so go for the shared pleasure. Once children make the story happen in their imagination, they have discovered the thrill of reading, and you won't be able to stop them. At that point, just go get them more books, and more comics.

TOON into Reading

LEVEL 1

FIRST COMICS FOR BRAND-NEW READERS

GRADES K–1 • LEXILE BR–100
GUIDED READING A–G • READING RECOVERY 7–10

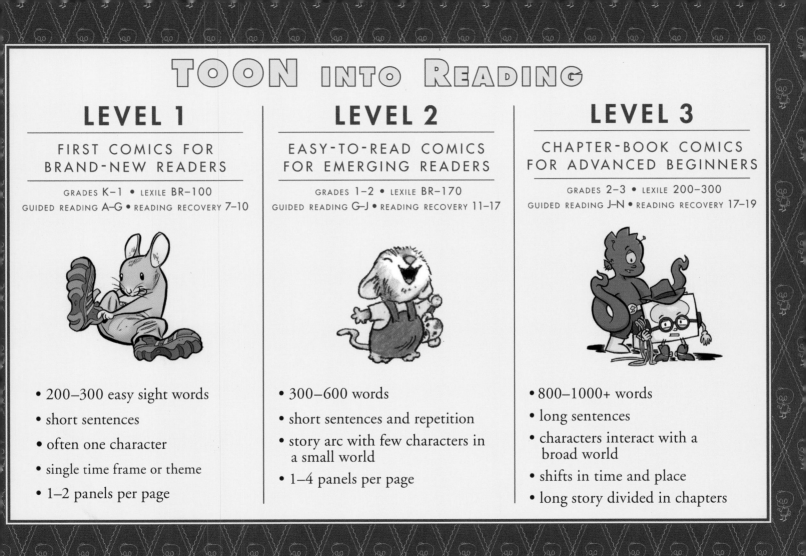

- 200–300 easy sight words
- short sentences
- often one character
- single time frame or theme
- 1–2 panels per page

LEVEL 2

EASY-TO-READ COMICS FOR EMERGING READERS

GRADES 1–2 • LEXILE BR–170
GUIDED READING G–J • READING RECOVERY 11–17

- 300–600 words
- short sentences and repetition
- story arc with few characters in a small world
- 1–4 panels per page

LEVEL 3

CHAPTER-BOOK COMICS FOR ADVANCED BEGINNERS

GRADES 2–3 • LEXILE 200–300
GUIDED READING J–N • READING RECOVERY 17–19

- 800–1000+ words
- long sentences
- characters interact with a broad world
- shifts in time and place
- long story divided in chapters